THE STONEMASON AND THE LADY

Dear Editor Book Two

EMILY SHARPE

Published by Blushing Books
An Imprint of
ABCD Graphics and Design, Inc.
A Virginia Corporation
977 Seminole Trail #233
Charlottesville, VA 22901

Emily Sharpe
The Stonemason and the Lady

Amazon ISBN: 978-1-64563-593-2
Barnes & Noble ISBN: 978-1-64563-594-9
Kobo ISBN: 978-1-64563-595-6
Apple ISBN: 978-1-64563-596-3
Print ISBN: 978-1-64563-597-0
Audio ISBN: 978-1-64563-598-7
v1

Dedicated to the fine writers of Use Your Words writing group, at the Inner Truth Project, in Port St. Lucie, Florida and to my first real editor—all of whom encouraged me to keep going.

Note from the Author

This is a work of fiction. Names, characters, business, events, and incidents are the products of the author's imagination. Some locations mentioned are in existence. Resemblance to actual persons or events is purely coincidental, but the author sincerely hopes that all of us find the kind of love and happiness that is possible.

It's never too late!

Bridesmaid Day

Eric stretched on the bed beside his fiancée, waking her. Donna opened her eyes to bright sunlight streaming through the white slatted blinds. *A beautiful fall morning and a wonderful day.* In a few hours, she would help her best friend prepare for her wedding and stand at the front of the church with her. She sighed at the thought.

"Penny for your thoughts?" Eric asked, turning over on his side and reaching up to brush an errant blonde curl from Donna's face. A strand of his long strawberry blonde hair fell in front of his shoulder.

Donna giggled and pulled the strand gently so that he would bring his mouth closer for a good morning peck. "I think you can afford more than a penny."

Eric shook his head so that the sunlight caught his thick hair and beard. He was clean-shaven when they'd first met a year ago, but he had grown it back, and then some. He kept things neat, but his handsome features reminded Donna of a Scottish laird of old. Sometimes she wished he would act more like a laird, more… forceful. She could easily see him in the cast of *Outlander*, and what she wouldn't give to play the maiden who caught his eye! *You've got a lot more than his eye*, her inner self chided.

"I need another job before that." Eric chuckled, not really worried. A talented stonemason, he'd recently finished one large job on the new city hall downtown, but nothing loomed on the horizon in the foreseeable future. "You'll find my life is one of feast or famine. Here in a bit, I'll have cycled back to famine. At least *you've* got a steady job, babe."

Donna wriggled from his embrace to get dressed, feeling his eyes on her as she walked to the closet for her robe. The bedroom was decorated for her and by her, in pastels and florals, feminine and completely suited to her perky disposition. The couple had consummated their relationship some months earlier in the room on the *other* side of the wall, however—the room where they had enjoyed quite a night of play just hours before. *That* room was decorated quite differently.

As Donna made a quick breakfast, Eric pulled on jeans and winced slightly. Donna's crop had been delightfully firm last night. Feeling the tenderness brought it all back, and he smiled as he readjusted himself in order to zip up the jeans. As much as he'd like to, he knew better than to call to Donna and suggest they return to bed in *either* room. She was on a mission. Bridesmaid Day was circled prominently on the calendar in the kitchen, and she had been counting down for weeks. There would be no time for an encore performance in the red room until late that night.

Pouring a steaming cup of coffee, Eric sat down in one of the dinette chairs and watched Donna move from cabinet to stove, to refrigerator and back. *Jessica's getting married today,* he thought. There had been a time when he had assumed that whenever that day came, *he* would be the one standing at the altar to meet her. They had dated a long time. They had seemed destined for marriage. Eric stared off into the distance, remembering.

Donna cleared her throat loudly. "Ahem. I can afford more than a penny."

Eric smiled and took a sip of his coffee. Just the way he liked it, black, no sweetener. "I was just thinking of the day we met."

Donna smiled as she expertly flipped the cheese omelet. "I was standing in line at the hot dog stand—"

"And you turned around and said hi because you are just naturally friendly, and I told you I'd come downtown to surprise my girlfriend for lunch, and then we—"

"Sat by the fountain and talked and laughed and ate our hot dogs and you told me you'd seen her with another man at a restaurant, so you didn't follow through, but—"

"I knew that something magic had happened when we met, and I broke up with Jessica that very night, over… if memory serves, a damn good pizza."

Donna slid the omelet onto a plate and brought it and two forks to the little table. Donna took a sip of Eric's coffee and wrinkled her nose before jumping back up to pour her own cup, doctoring it with copious amounts of cream and sugar before taking her seat again. "And I didn't know your last name and you didn't know mine, but somehow Jessica figured out that I was the girl you had met and were so delighted by and that you were the man I met and couldn't stop gushing over. She gave you my number, wished us well, said goodbye, and drove off into the sunset. Or to her apartment. One of those."

They clicked their coffee mugs together for a toast. "And I called you as soon as she left my apartment and the rest is history," Eric said. "I've never looked back, Donna. I've told you—there was *always* something missing with Jessica. She knew it; I knew it. We never talked about it, but we were definitely not on the same page."

Donna batted her long eyelashes over her upheld fork. "But we are!" *Well, almost.*

After dating chastely for several months, Eric had found Donna's notes one night for an article for the magazine at which both she and Jessica Daniels worked. *Our City* would profile an underground S&M club, one of those open secrets that no one bothers with unless there's a problem. While researching the article, Donna had been allowed to interview, visit, and photograph—all very discreetly. In the process, she discovered what had been missing in her own sex life, at least theoretically. She'd taken it no further than some planning and a few purchases—that is, until she led Eric into her red room that fateful night.

Months later, the red room was a regular "thing" for them. Last night had been a typical evening of rough play, with Donna as the dominatrix. In fact, after the first time, when Eric had dutifully and enthusiastically taken orders from her as she walked him through tying her up, whipping her with the crop, handcuffing her to the special bed in the red room, and finally making love to her, he seemed to be content with being the sub to her Domme. She enjoyed the fact that she was able to give him what he wanted, but lately, she found herself wishing he would take a more... *active*... role. *Oh well. No relationship is perfect. We'll sort it out.*

Unbidden, a thought came to mind. She'd kidded Jessica about wanting too much from a man, but deep down she hadn't wanted to settle for less than the very best, either. *Is that what I'm doing? Am I settling? Shouldn't I tell him what I want? How I feel? I am in the communication industry, after all.* She also realized that for most of her life, she had kept her truest, deepest feelings sheltered and protected, far from prying eyes and probing questions.

Eric was frowning. "Are you okay, babe?"

Nothing must spoil Bridesmaid Day. "Of course! More than okay. I think I'm just a little jittery about the ceremony. I want everything to be perfect for Jessica and Worth."

Eric leaned over and kissed her, tasting of cheese and coffee. "It will be, I have no doubt. The only people I've ever seen as happy together as those two are, are you and me. I'm glad you're going to be her maid of honor. There was a time I was afraid you might lose the friendship because of me, but look at you! Best friends, maid of honor. Think of it as a trial run when you're walking slowly down the aisle. It can be a practice run for our own wedding in a few months. Hopefully."

Donna covered her concerns with a quick smile. They had talked about getting married sometime after the first of the year, but just a week or so ago, she'd told Jessica they might move up the date. Eric was moving in with her soon—which was true—and she'd blurted to Jessica that they were going to be married just a few weeks after that. *Why did I do that? Do I not want her there? For all I know, their honeymoon will last an entire month.* Maybe they should go to the justice of the peace, anyway. No guests at all. But she'd always dreamed of a small ceremony, at least. Nothing fancy, but special.

First things, first. Get Jessica married. Move Eric in. We'll figure it out.

"What do you think?" Jessica Daniels twirled in front of the full-length mirror in the dressing area of the church. She wore a cowl-necked sheath of pure white. Jessica and Donna might be best friends and co-workers, perfectly suited in many ways, but there was not much resemblance in their appearance. Age-wise, yes, but while Jessica had an hourglass figure, generous bust, and flowing brown hair, Donna was more athletically built, slender, with a mass of unruly blonde curls.

Jessica's wedding gown was long sleeved—a good choice with autumn's chill outside. Each sleeve came to a point on the hand that reached all the way to the fingers in what Donna thought was quite striking and sophisticated. The back was low and also draped. There was a modest train. Donna would be worrying about tripping if it were her, but Jessica exuded nothing but confidence, poise, and joy.

Donna smiled at her friend's reflection in the mirror. "You look absolutely beautiful."

The other attendants were from Jessica's new family, now sisters by marriage: Kari and the increasingly pregnant Layla. Jessica's mother, a widow, had recently married a long-time friend, the city's newly retired fire chief—who was Kari's father and Layla's father-in-law. Chet Henderson would have the privilege of walking Jessica down the aisle. He'd known her since she was a little girl riding on her father's shoulders—a fellow firefighter who had perished in a blaze just two years earlier.

Kari acted as make-up artist and Donna had to admit, even though it was more makeup than she normally wore, each woman looked exquisite. Donna didn't know what half the items in Kari's make-up case were even called, but she had sat patiently and frozen, letting Kari brush here, powder there.

The attendants' differently-styled dresses were all made from the same teal silk by a local seamstress Worth's mother had recommended. As maid of honor, Donna's cowl-necked sheath most closely mirrored the bride's dress, but it fell just below the knees with a layered skirt. Kari's had a waist, puffed sleeves and full skirt, while Layla's empire waist gown accommodated her growing belly.

Layla giggled. "Thank you for not picking some god-awful color or design. I can actually wear this again. I feel like a princess." She did a little twirl herself, knocking over a lamp but catching it before it fell.

"Careful, little mama," Kari sighed. "You'll make my niece or nephew dizzy." She dearly loved her sister-in-law but sometimes she felt she had to mother her a bit.

There was a soft knock on the door before it opened. Carol Henderson entered, radiant in the same ivory lace dress in which she'd been wed some weeks before. Jessica had assured her that it would be completely appropriate for the day.

"Oh, ladies. You look wonderful!" Carol exclaimed. "I wanted to give my daughter one last hug before I'm seated." She threw her arms lovingly but carefully around Jessica. "I don't want to smudge your makeup, sweetheart—Kari, you should change vocations. You could be a make-up artist to the stars." She turned back to the bride. "I just wanted to hug you one final time as Jessica Daniels. When next we hug, you'll be Mrs. Vincent!" Normally calm and collected, Carol's face twisted into a happy but emotional mess.

"Don't cry, Mom, or you'll get me started too," Jessica said softly.

The other women instinctively backed up a few steps to give mother and daughter a little privacy in the small room, each one lost in thought. Each of them had lost their own mothers—Kari's mother had been Carol's friend for many years before dying of cancer. Layla's mother had died when she was quite young. And Donna's—*no, I won't even think about that today.*

"Your father would be so proud of you," Carol was saying. "He loved to talk about walking you down the aisle one day, but Chet is thrilled you asked him."

"'Help me with the veil?" Jessica smiled over to Kari, who was standing the closest. Her stepsister carefully removed the simple veil from its little stand and handed it to Carol, who gently rested it on Jessica's head.

They all oohed and ahhed before Carol squealed as she checked her wristwatch. "Yikes! It's time to start, ladies. I'd better go. Oh, and you will be impressed with the men. I stopped by to hug Worth before I came here, and they *all* look hot!"

They laughed as Carol left, leaving the door ajar so they could hear "their" music when the organist played it. The rehearsal had gone smoothly the night before and no one seemed particularly nervous, least of all the bride-to-be. Jessica had no second thoughts whatsoever, it appeared.

Watching her friend, Donna thought, *I hope I'll feel that way on my wedding day*. As Kari and Layla picked up their bouquets and took last minute looks in the mirror, Donna smoothed the back of Jessica's veil. Soon they would join Chet in the church's narthex and prepare for their grand entrance. Eric had already taken his seat on the bride's side, she was sure. He'd promised to sit where she could find him easily in the sea of faces. He'd known Jessica for so long, it made sense he'd want to be on her side.

Jessica didn't have a huge family, but all of their magazine co-workers, plus friends from school and former jobs, would be there for the joyous occasion. Worth's side would likely have fewer, but more exotic, guests. After a lifetime of traveling the globe to escape his troubled past, there might be any number of foreigners in the group.

"I'm so happy for you," Donna whispered to her friend. "Thank you for letting me be part of your special day."

Jessica directed a little air kiss to her so as not to muss her lipstick. "You were my first friend at the magazine, and you are my best friend ever, Donna Radford, soon-to-be-Donna-Brown. You've been with me from the beginning of our relationship—who *else* would be my maid of honor?"

"Remember the flowers?" Donna teased. "I thought they were from Eric, although I had no idea who 'Eric' was."

Almost a year ago to the day, Worth had sent a gorgeous vase of flowers to the magazine office where they worked—where he was the brand new editor, unbeknownst to them—along with a note of apology. Worth had crossed the line in a most delightful and passionate way, from what Jessica had finally divulged. Jessica had *thought* he was Eric at the time.

Donna gave a little smirk, remembering Jessica's implication that Eric was not passionate like the man she'd kissed in the darkness last Halloween at a party. "I should've known then that it wasn't Eric," she'd said.

He's passionate with me, *though. You would never guess the things we do in our red room. Never in a million years.* Maybe one day she'd show Jessica the room—not to brag about their relationship, certainly, but Donna was fiercely loyal. She wanted Jessica to know that Eric had grown, changed, that they were as well-suited for one another as Jessica and Eric had not been. It was obvious that Jessica still thought of Eric as being unemotional, a bit stiff. *Stiff indeed. Especially when I pull out the cuffs.* She laughed out loud.

"What's so—oh, there's your cue," Jessica said as the organist began playing *Clair de Lune.*

The ladies took a spontaneous deep breath in unison and stepped out into the narthex where Chet was waiting. As they approached, he held out his right elbow for Jessica to hold. "Ladies, you look lovely. Now let's get this show started."

First Kari, then Layla, began their journeys down the aisle. Ahead of them stood Worth, his administrative assistant Skip, and Skip's husband Paul, in gray suits with teal silk ties and handkerchiefs. *They really are hot,* Donna thought. *But not as hot as Eric!* As she walked down the aisle, her eyes darted this way and that, looking for the strawberry blonde head of hair that she loved.

There! As she approached the pew where Eric sat, he smiled at her and gave her a wink. He'd chosen to sit on the groom's side. *Well played, Eric. Well played.* If she'd thought he had any stubborn feelings for his former girlfriend, that settled things nicely.

Donna walked slowly toward the front, smiling at her boss,

Worth Vincent. He looked nothing like Eric, with his shaved head and neat goatee and mustache of dark brown. Eric's mop had gotten long enough that sometimes he wore it pulled back into a neat ponytail, as he did today, and his beard had grown back even redder than his hair. *And sometime next year, you'll be the groom standing at the front of the church,* Donna thought with pounding heart. *And I'll be the bride. I do hope Jessica can be there.*

Taking her place by Layla, she nodded to the organist, who flawlessly ended a strain of *Clair de Lune,* paused briefly for effect, and began the familiar strains of Mendelssohn's *Wedding March.* Donna felt like her heart would burst as Chet and Jessica began to walk down the aisle. In a few months, it would be her turn. A sudden thought interrupted the moment.

Who will walk me *down the aisle?*

2

New Guy at Work

Monday morning, Donna slept late again, scrambling to get ready for work. She was in no mood to stand in line for the copier, especially behind Karen in Human Resources—a notorious chatterbox. She'd heard three reports of Peeping Toms in the last month and wasn't that more than usual? She just hoped they caught the guy soon because she lived alone and didn't know what she would do if she saw someone looking through her window at night.

Looking at the woman finishing her task at a glacial pace, talking non-stop, Donna thought cattily that no one in his right mind would be hanging outside *her* window. *Honestly, can she move any slower?*

Paul took his place in line behind Donna, muttering something about Monday mornings. "Quite the wedding, though, eh?"

Reliving details of the weekend's wedding was a welcome distraction. "You and Skip looked very handsome," she said. "It really was a great evening."

"We thank you," the magazine photographer said with a

bow. "And you were every bit as beautiful as the bride yourself."

Donna giggled, rattling the papers in her hands. "Abu Dhabi," she said with awe. "Can you imagine honeymooning in Abu Dhabi?" Her eyes widened. "The photographs of the hotel Jessica and Worth are…" She glanced at her watch. "… flying to right now, in fact… it is gorgeous. Very modern. Very posh."

Paul laughed. "Very out of *our* league, I'm sure." Paul and Skip were both handsome fellows, in Donna's opinion, and they had all worked together long enough that Donna had been invited to their wedding some years earlier, shortly after the state laws regarding gay marriage had changed. "Don't get me wrong; I do some freelance work on the side and we're doing fine, but Jessica really did well for herself."

For some reason, his comment irritated Donna. Was he saying that she hadn't? That Eric couldn't provide for them? It made Jessica sound like a gold-digger. Never one to mask her feelings—*at least at work*, she thought briefly—Donna pivoted to face Paul. "Worth has a pile of money, but that's not at all why she married him."

Paul threw his hands up in mock horror. "I surrender. Jeez! That's not what I meant. It's obvious they're very much in love. And love is all that matters, Donnala."

Donna's cheeks reddened at his use of the pet name. "I'm sorry, Paul. A busy week, following some busy months. I'm just in a foul mood. I shouldn't have taken it out on you."

The pair stepped forward a few feet as the next co-worker in line got started at the copier. It had been quite the year, in fact. The city had struggled with arson—each fire set by a different arsonist, someone who perished in the fires by suicide —or so it was thought. Chief Henderson's top investigators were working hard when Jessica had suggested a specific person who might be the real culprit—a man who had falsely accused Worth of a murderous fire when they were both children.

Now that the mystery was solved, the entire city breathed a sigh of relief. Jessica had received an award for her part, and Chief Henderson had retired and married Jessica's mom. Chet's family had moved closer, Jessica and Worth were married now, people were selling houses and buying, and she and Eric were trying to save money.

Donna blew out a big breath. *Money. That must be why I'm on edge.* Aloud, she continued the apology. "Eric isn't working. Just finished one job, nothing ahead that we know of. Weather's getting colder soon, so outdoor construction has a way of drying up." Donna shrugged and made herself smile, hoping it was convincing. "It'll be fine. Nothing a cup of coffee wouldn't help, anyway."

Paul nodded. "Something'll turn up, I'm sure. Oh, but speaking of photographs, we have a new photographer. Just started today. Skip's running around like a chicken with his head cut off since the boss is honeymooning, or he'd probably introduce him to everyone. Skip does love to get hold of that microphone."

It was now Donna's turn at the copier. As she worked, she stretched her back. Tonight, she planned to insist on the red room, hoping that Eric would agree to a role reversal. It wasn't that she minded being the Domme. She knew that a lot of couples at the club—from when she'd interviewed them for the article, with the strict promise not to photograph faces or print names—believed that staying in one role was better. That was the traditional thought... if S&M could ever be called *traditional*.

Some, though, like herself—and she hoped, Eric—enjoyed changing roles, being what was appropriately called a "switch". It kept things fresh, or she thought it would. Donna had only just researched and outfitted the red room when she and Eric met. After their first time there, the night she talked Eric through being the dominant, he'd wanted to be the sub. It was okay, but did they want to settle for okay? *Do I?* Sometimes she lay awake, thinking about planning for a wedding in a few months, followed by a lifetime together. Did she want to be the Domme... forever?

"Speak of the devil," Paul said, bringing Donna back to the present. A man approached, someone Donna had never seen before. He was dressed casually, with one of those multi-pocketed fishing vests some photographers favor. "This is the new photographer I was telling you about. Donna Radford, meet Lance Glover. Donna, Lance. Lance, Donna."

Lance Glover was not as handsome as Eric, she thought loyally, but he was easy enough on the eyes. There was something about him that was oddly familiar. Dark-haired and swarthy, Lance swept his eyes up and down, assessing Donna in such a frank way that she was a bit offended and also, she had to admit, flattered. As busy as she was, though, she only managed a limp squeeze when he held out his hand.

Lance chuckled good-naturedly. "Surely, you can do better than that for a first handshake." To get her to squeeze harder, he increased his own pressure, to the point that it hurt.

Macho man. This wasn't the morning for such things, but there was no way this stranger would realize it. Donna's eyes narrowed as she withdrew her hand abruptly. Something flickered in his eyes as she did, and his smile faded just as abruptly.

Donna finished her work and gathered her copies. She really did need that cup of coffee. She'd snapped at Paul and now she'd offended the new guy. *Great start to the day.* "I'm sorry. I hope you'll be happy here at the magazine. Mr. Vincent—Worth—was focused on finishing up things before the wedding and honeymoon. Otherwise, I'm sure he would have told everyone you were coming today."

"I'd love to be... *coming* today," Lance said, lowering his voice so suggestively that Paul snickered. "But it could still happen. The day is young."

In answer to the obvious come-on, Donna simply walked away, hoping she was accomplishing something between storming and strutting. *The nerve of the guy. Jerk.* She was sure that Lance hadn't displayed that particular side of himself at his interview; Worth was one of the last true gentlemen on the planet. He wouldn't want that kind of thing at the magazine if he could help it. Lord knows, he'd kept Jessica on a roller coaster ride for much of their relationship, wanting to keep things proper and above-board at the office.

Maybe it's just first day jitters. I've got money jitters and wedding jitters. I suppose he's allowed.

By mid-afternoon, Donna's mood had improved greatly. Although she'd missed Jessica's company at lunch—Worth was usually otherwise engaged at noon, so the friends enjoyed that time together—Donna had gotten a great deal accomplished. She was ahead of deadlines and had several ideas to pitch when Worth returned. She could afford to slow her pace and chat with co-workers, their conversations mostly centered on the wedding. The reception, the food, everything had been first-rate.

Eric called her cell phone just as she was packing up to leave for the day, at five. "Babe, I've got news!" he said breathlessly.

Donna set her purse and backpack on her office chair. "Well, what?" She grinned in anticipation.

"I'll tell you tonight." His voice dropped in volume. "Maybe you should tie me up first and *make* me."

Donna sighed. So much for suggesting a role reversal. "Just tell me."

Eric recognized the edge in her voice, although it wasn't heard often. Usually positive and perky, she clearly had had a less than stellar day. He might pay for that later. *Not necessarily a bad thing,* he thought. His voice lightened. "I will; I promise. But I called to see if you'd like me to bring take-out or if you planned for us to cook?"

"Take-out, please. Anything you want is fine," Donna said. "Love you." She slipped her phone into the pocket of her purse and headed for the door. She was ready for a hot shower and maybe a nap.

In the hall, she was irritated to see Lance waiting for the elevator. She glanced around, hoping someone else would join them. "Did you have a good first day?" she said cheerfully, hiding her displeasure at the thought of being alone with him. *I should give him the benefit of the doubt.*

Lance smiled without even the hint of a leer. "I did; thanks for asking." He held up his bag. "Headed for the gym. Not the best way to work off calories, but it'll do in a pinch."

Judging from his earlier comment, Donna felt she could guess which calorie-burner he preferred, but there was nothing suggestive in his tone. *Maybe I'm just reading something into it. In a pinch, he says. Just let him try.*

The elevator doors opened and the two stepped in. Donna stayed as far to one side as she could without appearing rude. Lance pulled out his phone and scrolled through several screens. Neither spoke until the elevator came to a stop.

So, nothing to worry about after all, Donna thought with relief. Still, she headed straight for the water fountain in the building's lobby and waited until Lance had walked outside the front doors, headed—she assumed—to the gym next door before she turned and walked to the parking garage for her car.

3

News and New Things

Donna licked an errant drop of duck sauce from her lip, moaning with delight. "Chinese hit the spot, Eric." She'd had time for a long, hot shower before he let himself in to catch her napping on the couch. Dressed only in lacy underthings, she had headed for the closet, only to be stopped by his dramatic wail of complaint.

"Nooo," he'd called after her. "No need to dress on *my* account."

Laughing, she had done an about-face and run to embrace him. "I can do that. Or not do that, I mean."

Now they sat across from each other at the little table, finishing a delicious meal of bourbon chicken and egg rolls, accompanied by ice cold beers. Donna waited until Eric sat back in his chair, his meal devoured, before she raised the topic of his news.

"Well," he began slowly. "It's *good* news." He frowned. "Maybe a hint of bad news mixed in. Surprising news, at any rate." He paused. "It's a job. A good one. High paying. High paying, like 'I've never been so well paid for one job ever in my *life*' high paying."

Donna squealed and clapped her hands. "That's great!" She jumped up to wriggle onto his lap, kissing him sweetly all over his face. "I'm so proud of you. And you were worried. I knew something would come up, Eric. You're an artist with stonework. I was sure the city hall project would open doors for you."

Eric held her tightly then looked up at her with a frown. "Ready for the bad news?"

"Oh, right. You did warn me," she said, preparing herself mentally. "Shoot."

"The job's not local. It's in Florida. A custom fireplace, floor to ceiling—a very high ceiling, I gather. It will take some time."

Donna smirked. "What's so bad about that?"

Eric gently pushed her off his lap so that he could stand. He began to pace around the kitchen as he talked. "They want me to start soon, in order to finish the job before January first. I'll be the only one working—they'll put me up at the house, feed me, pay for my flight. But I have to leave right away."

"Tomorrow?"

Eric stopped, shaking his head. "Before Thanksgiving, though. They definitely want me there before Thanksgiving."

Donna scrunched her shoulders up, thinking. "That gives us… almost three weeks? You were going to move in this weekend so the timing's good in that regard."

Eric nodded. "I'd like you to consider something else, babe." Ever since the phone call from Florida, he'd been worried about leaving Donna. They'd had a great year, but maybe that had been because they'd spent so much time together. He was concerned. Donna was a prize. She was currently *his* prize, but what if someone else, someone better, came along? He'd rather not find out the hard way that that old saying 'absence makes the heart grow fonder' wasn't really accurate.

Eric stretched out his arms, and she melted into them. "Would you be willing to move the wedding up?"

Donna looked up at him, amazed. "Willing? Of course, I'm willing! The only reason we were waiting was to save money, right? And you're going to make *beaucoup* bucks now." A thought made her laugh out loud. "Oh my god, you won't believe this. I actually blurted to Jessica that we were getting married before Thanksgiving—I don't know where that came from. But maybe she'll be back in time after all. Anyway, it doesn't matter. Let's do it!"

"Speaking of 'doing it'," Eric grinned, tracing one finger down her neck to tease the small mound inside her bra, "we can talk wedding plans soon enough. Right now, I'd like to practice for the honeymoon." He tilted his head toward the closed door of the red room. "In there, please."

Donna took him by the hand and led him inside, closing the door and lighting candles as he undressed. *I'm getting married. Not in months, but in weeks. This man loves me, and tonight, he gets exactly what he wants, and then some. Time to try out some new toys.*

Eric stood by the specially made bed, completely nude. Stonemasons must be strong for their work, and Donna gazed greedily at the way the candlelight danced over his muscular physique. She thought back to their first night together, how she'd wanted him to make love to her with his clothes on— well, mostly on.

It was something she thought about often, her fantasy of being naked, vulnerable, being taken by a handsome man who happened upon her as she... what? Bathed in a pond in the moonlight? Found a stranger in the dark, the way Worth had "found" Jessica at that Halloween party last year? *No matter. It'll keep.* Tonight, was about celebrating Eric and his news. Her fantasy could wait.

Walking to the closet, she pulled out a plastic sheet she'd

tucked away. Handing it to Eric, she ordered, "Spread this out on the bed, then lie face down on it."

He obeyed as she watched. "This is new…" he murmured as he lay down.

"I bought some special candles; the wax will be hot when I drip it on your skin. And then you might want to return the favor." She pulled out the soft restraints, rather than metal handcuffs, pulled his arms above his head and secured his hands to the bar at one end of the bed, his ankles to the other. "I love candles, don't you?" She tipped the candle slightly so that hot wax dripped onto the small of his back.

"Ouch!" Eric's body recoiled from the sudden heat, but couldn't move away.

Donna dripped the special melted wax again along his back, at the small of his knees, onto his neck, his wrists. He winced each time, but Donna sensed his mounting pleasure in the little gasps he made. "Good! Now rest your head and wait," she said as she rotated it.

After a few minutes, she removed the restraints and smiled at him. "I hope you liked that, Eric." She stroked his back gently. "Would you turn over now?" Donna tied his wrists above his head once more.

His erection throbbed in the candlelight; his chest rose and fell quickly with desire. Donna straddled his feet, then rose on her knees so that he could watch her remove her panties. She inched her way up onto him and held the panties over his face. "Can you smell me? Do you like that?"

Eric moaned a little as he nodded. She knew that what he wanted was for her to slip down onto his cock, to bring on the climax he was aching to experience. "Not just yet," she whispered. Maybe if she asked him outright, he would let her experience the same sensations. "Would you like to use the candle on me now?

"Oh, baby. I can't wait much longer."

Donna bit her lip, reminding herself that this was a celebration of his good news. Continuing her climb, she stopped when her little triangle of blonde fur was positioned just over his face. "Pleasure me," she said, lowering herself just enough that his tongue and lips could begin. He would want to caress her buttocks, but he could not. He would want to be inside of her instead, but he could not.

Delicately, his tongue explored every fold of her mound, toying with her little button. When he twirled his tongue and wrapped his lips around her clitoris, she began to rock gently, her inner thighs tickled by his beard. Only when she had reached her climax, did she slide down onto his cock and sit perfectly still, feeling its heat and hardness, forcing him to lie still when every ounce of his being wanted to buck up and down like a bronco so that he could have his own release.

"Shall I let you go now?" Donna teased sternly.

Eric nodded.

"I think not," she said. "I think you must be quiet and still a little longer."

Abruptly, she sat up and, in one swift motion, turned around so that her buttocks were near his face. She took his cock into her mouth and sucked hard. Before he could climax, she released him. This time, she bit him, first gently, then harder, then lowered her mouth to his scrotum, licking his balls gently. "Shall I bite you there too?"

Eric winced at the thought but said nothing, fearing that she would do just that if he disobeyed.

Donna nibbled along his inner thighs down to his feet, biting each toe tip while one hand masterfully kneaded his penis, released, then kneaded again. She would not allow him to climax, not yet. He would explode inside of her and nowhere else. Sensing that he could not hold it off any longer, she whipped around and lowered herself onto his cock as she released his hands so that he could finally touch her, hold her.

21

With one deep thrust, he was there. He let out a long cry of satisfaction and relaxed.

"Oh, don't you even think of it," Donna said. "I'm not done with you yet." Wildly, she rocked atop him. Happy to give her more, Eric grasped her bottom and pulled her tighter as she rode the wave of ecstasy again, and yet again. Finally, she laid her head on his chest. "Whew," she sighed. "Well done."

Eric rolled her off him and onto the mattress, kissing her gently. "You were amazing. *That* was amazing. A little freaky there for a second, with the hot wax, but amazing." He lay beside her; they listened to the sound of their own breaths and watched the reflection of the candlelight flickering on the metal bars of the bed. After a while, Eric propped his weight onto one elbow and played with the lace on her bra. "Do many subs get to marry their Dommes?" he mused.

Donna smiled. "I suppose if they tell them to, they do." She giggled. "But you asked me, not the other way around." *Tell me to marry you now, Eric. Dominate me. Take me again.*

"Let's go to sleep now, babe," Eric said, rolling off the bed and blowing out the candles. "I'll tidy up in the morning."

Donna closed her eyes. It had been a spectacular evening. The new job, the money it represented, moving the wedding up, trying out new things. There was no earthly reason for her to want more.

Reason has nothing to do with it, whispered her mind. *And you* do *want more.*

4

Plans All Around

The next several nights were filled with packing. Eric complained that he'd be packing twice—first for the move to Donna's apartment and then for the adventure in Florida. "Maybe I should just stay here until after the flight," he suggested while taping up a box, "and you could pack it all up to take home with you." While he wasn't serious, she knew he'd rather do it that way.

Donna stood up with her hands on her hips, incredulous. "Are you kidding? You've *got* to be kidding. This is *your* stuff! I'm not doing all the work. When would I have time?"

Eric pulled a marker from behind his ear and labeled the box. "Once I leave town, you'll have a lot more time than you do now. No boyfriend to tie up, no butt to whip…"

Donna giggled as she worked. "I could find somebody, I'm sure." Glancing at Eric, she saw the look on his face. "Now *I'm* kidding, you big goof. Besides, by then you won't be my boyfriend, you'll be my husband."

She watched as Eric carried the box out into the living room with the rest of the stacks. Calling after him, she said, "I was thinking about a part-time job. We could save even faster."

Eric said something she couldn't hear. "What was that?" she sang as she carried a box for him to stack.

Eric took the box from her, then he took her in his arms. "I said the magazine keeps you plenty busy, I thought, but maybe something else for nights and weekends isn't such a bad idea. You could take up tennis. Or scrapbooking. A hobby to keep my wife out of trouble."

"Out of trouble or away from other men? You know there are a lot of men at the office," she teased.

Eric kissed the top of her head. "Skip and Paul are great—hang out with them when you miss the smell of aftershave."

Donna giggled. "There are some straight men at the office too. Worth, Frank, Lance…" Just saying the new photographer's name was unreasonably distasteful.

"Why the face? And who's Lance? I don't remember hearing that name before," Eric said as he went back to work.

As Donna tucked socks and underwear into another box, cushioning some framed photos she added to the box, she regaled Eric with the whole bad-mood-meeting-Lance day. She hadn't talked with the man since they were on the elevator. As far as she knew, he was helping Paul on assignment and working on some special photo shoot as a side gig. "Apparently, he hasn't told anyone what he's shooting, or where, just that he takes it very seriously. We're all supposed to be quite impressed, too." She rolled her eyes as she worked.

Eric tried to sound disinterested when he asked for a description. *He's jealous!* "Oh he's very handsome," she teased. "Like a movie star. Seriously, though, he's okay. Dark hair, dark complexion. You know how a person can remind you of someone else? Universal looks. Nothing that really stands out." *Except his innuendos.* A few of the other women had complained among themselves, which was actually a relief to Donna. At least he hadn't singled her out for his unwanted attentions.

Eric reached high for something at the top of his closet. His hair was loose, cascading onto his shoulders. *Lance is no match for my Eric*, Donna thought. Maybe a little time apart would make him want to be a bit more aggressive, more "take charge", but she also knew that she'd miss him terribly. Just the thought of the upcoming separation brought tears to her eyes.

When she sniffled, Eric turned around. "My high school baseball trophy!" He held up a small gold figurine atop a base. "I was a pretty good hitter."

Donna wiped her nose on the edge of her t-shirt and bent over provocatively in front of him. "Maybe now that you're not a hitter, you could be a *spanker*..." she purred.

In answer, Eric swatted her behind as he walked past to pack the trophy. "No time now, that's for sure. But the end is in sight."

He was right. They had so much to do before he left, with not long in which to accomplish it. She'd texted Jessica today to let her know the new wedding date, immediately receiving a barrage of happy emoticons from across the globe. The honeymoon was obviously going well.

She also texted Carol, who'd become a sort of mother figure recently, checking in to see how she was. Carol had been pretending last month, she was sure, when she said she needed Donna's help moving into the new condo she and Chet found. "Family" wasn't something Donna had experienced in a very long time, and she drank it all in like a thirsty sponge.

Eric and Donna decided to have a small chapel ceremony, with just a few of their closest friends. Jessica and Worth, and Carol and Chet, of course. The six of them had talked about all going out to dinner after Abu Dhabi, but now, there might not be time. Eric's personality didn't lend itself to having a lot of friends, but he did want to include a few guys who'd worked with him on the city hall job.

Donna had stopped by the job a few times, surprised at how friendly and open Eric was with the laborers, how authoritative he was. She'd thought about it a lot since—maybe he enjoyed being a sub all the time because at work, everything was his responsibility.

I'd like to be the sub for the same reason, Donna mused. *I've been in charge of everything in my life for so long. It would be nice to follow his lead for a change. Give it time.*

It was the next night when Eric brought up the idea of a hobby or second job to Donna. "Do you have any ideas? I don't know how I feel about you being out alone at night. Or even here alone at night, for that matter. I hope they catch the peeper soon." Four other women had filed reports, according to the evening news. Eric walked over to the bedroom window and pulled down the shade. "You never know."

"No, leave it up! Without sunlight, I'll never wake up in the morning." They were both exhausted, but the packing was almost done.

Eric let the shade back up then watched from the bed in Donna's room as she sat at a dressing table, brushing her curls. "Hobby? Job?"

"Well," she said, putting down the brush as she swiveled around to face him. "The club has an opening."

"The club? What club... oh. *That* club." Eric's eyes widened. Their first night together had followed a frank discussion of Donna's research for the article on the S & M club in town. Very hush-hush from all outward appearances, but apparently, business was booming.

"Everything is handled with the utmost discretion," Donna explained, "so the owner's extremely picky, even nervous, about new hires. She called the other day, though, thanking me again for the article—it came out months ago, but people are still making inquiries on her website because of it. Her numbers have really shot up." Donna made a little face. "But going from a few couples getting together to live out their fantasies is quite different than running an actual business. There are fees, rules, check-in and check-out. She runs a tight ship."

"I'll bet she does," Eric said dryly. "I'll bet she can really crack a whip, too."

Donna threw her brush at him. "Businesswoman first, dominatrix second. Anyway, she's gotten so busy with the business side, she hasn't had time for, well, doing what she does best, apparently. She's added rooms, renovated, hired someone to manage the website. For something so "secret", it's gotten pretty popular. And while she thanked me for providing objective, positive information for the community, she'd love to have me work there."

Immediately, Eric's face drained of color. "You mean you'd... to someone else... no! I won't have it!"

Donna sat beside him on the bed and held his hand sweetly. "Of course not. *Never*. That's just for you. You know, like that card you gave me—*any time, any place, any way, only you.* I would handle clerical duties, to take some of the load off her. That's all, babe."

Eric took a deep breath and said nothing, but he looked calmer.

Donna laid her head on his shoulder. "Do you remember the night you proposed? At that little Italian restaurant?"

The memory threw them both into a fit of chuckling. Eric had made reservations at a quaint bed and breakfast—so quaint and old that the walls were paper thin. On top of that, the inn was full of other guests they decided didn't need to wonder about the whip sounds or athletic lovemaking that was their norm. Their weekend had not been nearly as *active* as they would have preferred, but the proposal made their quite different kind of restraint that weekend all worthwhile.

Donna continued when she could catch her breath. "I told you then, remember? My toast? 'To the man of my dreams, the *yin* to my *yang*, the Dom to my sub and the sub to my Domme. May you always, always be in my life.'"

"I remember," Eric said softly. "If you want to work at the club, I don't mind. But just while I'm away, I hope."

Donna got up to turn out the light. Tonight, all she wanted was a snuggle and some sleep; she had a feeling that would be fine with Eric. She grinned in the darkness as she slithered between the sheets and curled up next to him, rolling her eyes. He had started wearing boxers and a t-shirt to bed, for some reason. Maybe he was just too tired to finish undressing. She pressed her firm breasts into his back, in case he still had any energy or desire.

"'Night," he mumbled.

Donna turned over and lay awake, wondering what an entire life with Eric would be like. It was what she wanted, but she'd seen little evidence of happy marriages in the past. Her mother had left when she was six, dying of an overdose a few years later. She'd chosen addiction rather than taking care of her daughter and husband. Donna's father had been ill-equipped for raising a daughter; that was certain. She moved those memories to another place in her mind—a bleak place—where she wouldn't have to face them now.

Jessica and Worth seem to really have it together, she mused. So did Carol and Chet and Chet's kids. Skip and Paul even, seemed quite content and happy. For all her bravado, though, Donna had doubts. Not so much about Eric's love and commitment, but about her ability to communicate what she wanted and needed from him. Quoting Scarlett O'Hara, she mumbled, "I'll think about that tomorrow," and fell asleep.

Sometime during the night, though, Donna sat bolt upright in bed with a loud scream, waking Eric. "What is it?" he cried, wrapping his arms tightly around her.

Donna was shaking, damp with perspiration. The dream had been so real, but now she could only remember snatches of the horror. "A man, Eric. I couldn't see his face, but I knew he wanted to do something terrible. I was running, trying to get away…" In spite of the dream, she suddenly snorted. "Good grief!"

Eric was confused. "What?"

Donna shook her head in the pre-dawn light of a bright moon outside her window. "I went to sleep thinking of Scarlett O'Hara and then dreamed that whole scene in *Gone with the Wind* where she's running in the mist. That's all it was. I'm sorry I woke you."

The two settled back into the bed. Eric was asleep within seconds, but Donna lay awake, trying to remember more of the dream's details. A man peering around a corner, but who? Donna closed her eyes and forced herself to think of kittens. *And the beach. And kittens at the beach.*

5

Bride and Groom Day

I t was a lovely Saturday afternoon. Autumn's paintbrush had outdone itself in the trees around the wedding chapel. A small gathering sat on the navy cushioned pews while a four-piece flute ensemble entertained them. Mr. and Mrs. Worth Vincent held hands as they waited. On the front row, where a bride's family would usually sit, Jessica's mother Carol and her brand new husband Chet had, at Donna's request, the place of honor. The Hendersons had also invited the new couple and guests to enjoy a light buffet at their condo after the ceremony.

At one o'clock sharp, the flute choir began the familiar strains of Pachelbel's *Canon* as Eric and Donna walked down the aisle together toward the front.

Jessica caught Donna's eye as she approached and smiled at her friend, mouthing the words "beautiful." It was true. Donna's blonde curls were golden in the sunlight streaming through the windows of the chapel.

She had been thrilled when Jessica presented her with a gown she'd purchased at a boutique in Abu Dhabi as a wedding present. Off-white, with a lace bodice and three-quarter length sleeves, the dress's simple lines were flattering to Donna's slim figure, and Jessica had guessed exactly right about the size. The hem reached just to her ankles, revealing boots of softest cream leather. Rather than a veil, she had a wreath of white flowers in her hair and carried a simple bouquet.

Eric's hair was pulled back into a neat pony tail that accentuated his bushy red beard. Handsome, in a navy suit, he was obviously pleased by the turn-out, nodding at friends. When his eye caught Jessica's, he made a "yikes" face—they'd never even *talked* about marriage, not seriously, yet here he was, just a few weeks after Jessica and Worth had tied the knot. Jessica gave him a little salute and a wink to signify her approval.

The quartet's music faded as Eric and Donna took their places in front of the officiant the chapel had assigned for the occasion, a tall woman with short gray hair decked out in a navy robe and white satin stole. "Dearly beloved," she began.

Jessica squeezed Worth's hand beside her. She was so pleased that Donna and Eric had found one another. The two couples had not spent much time together, but she hoped that would change. There was no awkwardness between Jessica and Donna, certainly. And there was no need for any between Worth and Eric, despite the fact that both had seen her naked. Jessica's cheeks flushed at the thought. It had taken a long time for her and Eric to become intimate, and compared to her experience with Worth, "intimate" really didn't adequately describe the relationship. There had always been a key factor missing. Eric hadn't been as… desirous… as she had been, for sure.

But Donna was obviously very happy, and that's all that mattered. Jessica would return to work on Monday, and from the sounds of it, so would Donna—no time for a honeymoon with all the preparations and plans before Eric left for Florida. Donna had told her friend that she had a surprise for him, though. When pressed for details, however, Donna had made a zipping motion with her mouth, her eyes sparkling. "One day, I'll dish, but not yet."

"This is delicious," Donna said. "Thank you so much for doing this, Carol." She took another bite of her shrimp taco, careful to eat over the plate as they stood on the condo's glassed-in porch. Outside, the sun was just dipping below the tall buildings and trees in the distance, bathing the whole scene in an amber glow.

Carol sipped her champagne. "We were happy to, Donna. You've been a wonderful friend to Jessica this year. And what a year it's been!"

Donna's eyes were round. "Amen to that." She looked around the room and into the main section of the condo, where friends snacked and chatted in little groups. "I really appreciate this; you have no idea. There wasn't time to move Eric to my place, get him packed for Florida, make arrangements with the chapel *and* worry about a reception." *Other than the private one a little later,* she thought.

Chet walked out to freshen their drinks. "Guess who just called? Keith says that Layla's having some issues, nothing serious. They're still planning to come for Thanksgiving dinner next week."

Carol nodded pleasantly. "Good, good—oh, Donna! Please join us for Thanksgiving! We don't have a table inside that's big enough for everyone to fit, but we'll pull some together out here if it's not too cold. And if it is, we'll just make do in there. Please say yes. Eric will be gone."

Donna looked across the porch where Eric and Worth were deep in discussion about something. The thought of spending another Thanksgiving alone was not appealing; there had been many in her life. In fact, she couldn't remember the last time she'd had a family Thanksgiving at all. The last one must have been with her father, just before she ran away for good.

"I'd be delighted, Carol," Donna said with a smile. "Let me know what I can bring."

By the time everyone left the Hendersons', the sun had turned the sky to red. Mr. and Mrs. Brown thanked the Hendersons one last time and drove off, literally, into the sunset. As Eric turned the wheel in the direction of their apartment, he yawned loudly.

"It's been a tiring few weeks, hasn't it?" Donna said.

Eric nodded with a smile as he drove. "Tiring, but fantastic." He glanced at her. "We're married, Donna! Sorry we can't have a honeymoon yet, but after Florida, we'll do something special. I appreciate how easy you've made this for me—not many brides would agree to a bit of a rush job, then say goodbye to the groom a few days later."

Donna put her hand on Eric's thigh. "We can FaceTime every day," she said. "And I could visit at Christmas if everyone's okay with that."

"They'll have to be," Eric said. "No way can I be away from you more than a month at a time. If the Steins don't have room at their house for us to be together, we'll get a hotel room." He lifted her hand to his lips for a kiss. "But not a quaint old bed and breakfast with thin walls!"

Donna laughed. "Exactly. Oh, turn right at the light, babe."

Eric obliged her, assuming she needed to make a stop at a store before they went home. "We're a little overdressed for the drug store," he teased.

"Actually," she said slowly. "Pull over. I want to drive."

"Oookay," he said. "I've married a woman of mystery, have I?"

Before she pulled back into traffic, Donna reached over his

lap and pulled something out of the glove compartment. "Put this on."

It was a blindfold. As he complied, Eric chuckled. "Well, I know you're not going to drive me to a brand new house, unless you won the lottery and forgot to tell me. That would be some wedding gift, though."

Donna giggled as she eased into the traffic flow but said nothing for several blocks. She pulled into the parking lot of a nondescript brick building whose windows and front double doors were covered with plywood and security bars. From all appearances, it was deserted, but Donna had a key. "You can get out now. I'll lead you from here."

At the door, Donna opened it and pulled Eric inside before locking the door behind herself. She entered a code to shut off the alarm system then turned on a soft light. The club was deserted—unusual for a Saturday evening, but Donna had made special arrangements with the owner. Her wedding night gift to Eric would be an introduction—for both of them, really —to all that the club had to offer. And as much as Donna would have enjoyed spending her wedding night fulfilling one of her own fantasies, this was her gift to Eric.

She led Eric to the biggest room she had toured. "Keep the blindfold on for now," she said.

Eric shook his head. "I have a feeling we're not in Kansas anymore," he quipped. "May I sit down, at least?"

Donna led him to a chair and helped him settle into it. "I'll only take a minute to change, babe."

When she removed his blindfold, however, she was no longer Donna, the beautiful bride in lace and flowers. He gasped and grinned. "This is the club?" he asked.

"The club."

The room was twice the size of their red room at home. A contraption Eric had never seen before hung from the ceiling. There was a bed similar to their own. Metal rings protruded from the walls at various heights, and strange equipment of all imaginable shapes was scattered around. There were no candles, but red light bulbs gave the room an unmistakable sensuality.

Donna was a vision in black, from the hood of her cape to her thigh-high leather boots. She wore a buckled corset with a halter closure over a short full skirt. The halter's cupless design gave the illusion of bigger breasts than she actually had, but when Eric leaned forward instinctively to kiss them, she stepped back. "Not so fast." She tilted her head toward the far wall, where a big X could be seen in the low light.

Eric wondered how he'd missed it before, or perhaps he had subconsciously dismissed it, assuming it was decorative. "That's a St. Andrew's Cross, isn't it?" *Hardly seems the place*, he thought.

"Just think of it as the X in 'sex' for our purposes. Now strip."

Eric shook his head in delighted amazement at his new bride's preparations. "How did you—"

Donna stepped so close to him that he could smell her breath. "This is not the time for pleasantries, sub. Unless you'd like to switch roles. As the Dom, you can do anything you want, including chitchat." *Yes, yes, this would be a great time to switch!* Donna's heart began to race at the thought. *And on our wedding night, the perfect time and place.*

But Eric threw up his hands in surrender and began taking off his clothes. Silently and carefully, he stripped, feeling more vulnerable than usual in the larger room. Their red room was close quarters, but this—it crossed his mind that he wasn't entirely sure what to expect. Donna had never let their times together get stale or predictable, but space constraints alone had been limiting. That would not, he understood, be the case tonight.

Donna had never used the club equipment, although she

had often thought of how lovely it would be for them to experience it together. In her fantasies, Eric took charge. Perhaps in time, but their wedding night was too precious to spoil with requests he was apparently not ready for.

For the next hour, Donna took her cues from her new husband, giving him exactly what he wanted, the way he wanted it, experimenting with first one apparatus or toy and then another. Her excitement grew as his did until she couldn't delay their gratification any longer. "There's another room I want to show you," she said. "Take me there?"

Eric picked her up in his strong arms. "You're the boss." His face was filled with so much love, Donna's heart swelled. One day he would understand her better, she hoped, but for now, this was her wedding night and she planned to enjoy herself.

She had already prepared the room. Decorated in purple and black, a circular water bed was the only furniture. Eric let her down gently, and she removed the cape. Everything else stayed on. At the questioning look Eric gave her, Donna smiled seductively and lay on her back, spreading her legs as she lifted the skirt. She was nude beneath it. In a moment, he was on top of her, inside of her, the waves of the bed providing an entirely new but very pleasant sensation.

Donna's back arched as a wave lifted her. Another wave sent her legs flying into the air. She wrapped the boots around Eric's waist as he thrust deeper and deeper until the only waves they were aware of were those of shared ecstasy.

The sensations stilled as their bodies relaxed. Donna could feel his cock soften within her, but she needed more. "Move very gently into me," she whispered. "Rock. Softly. Softly." She could feel his pubic bone teasing her at just the right spot. He might be done, but she was not. Her heat began to rise again, very slowly. He was barely moving against her, but it was enough. She had never felt such an intense orgasm. Usually, she was all about force and strength, more fucking, less making love. This was different. This was absolute bliss. She screamed with pleasure as her legs tightened around Eric again.

The sun was still low in the eastern sky as Donna and Eric walked almost shyly to the car to head back to the apartment. Throughout the night, they had experimented in various rooms. Between the sex, they had talked, discussed what this object might do, or what that equipment was for. They'd speculated about who might be members, who they would *never* see there, not in a million years. Some of the contrivances sent them into fits of giggles, but others—Eric's obvious appreciation for Donna's wedding gift was gratifying.

But if it had entered Eric's mind to try something of a more dominant nature on their wedding night, it had not been evident. He enjoyed being the sub. Donna enjoyed being the Domme. She made sure that she got every bit as much out of their encounters as he did, if not more. *One day, though,* she thought as she began to doze a little in the car. *One day, he will want to please me as much as I want to please him. And that will be a very good thing.*

6

Florida

"Hey, thanks for the lift, Chet," Eric said as shook the man's hand before getting out at the airport curb.

Chet gave Eric's hand a squeeze then popped the trunk remotely. "My pleasure, young man. Donna would've been a puddle of tears saying goodbye—no need for her to try to drive like that. And don't worry; we'll keep tabs on her while you're gone."

Eric nodded and said goodbye, pulling his luggage out of the trunk and slamming it closed. With a final wave to Chet, he headed inside. Ari Stein had booked him a nonstop flight to Orlando in first class; the Steins' chauffeur would pick him up for the two-hour drive to the coast.

Eric checked his larger bag and proceeded through security. The week before Thanksgiving, traffic had not yet picked up, so there wasn't much of a line.

"Where are *you* headed, handsome?" a feminine voice asked from behind him.

Eric turned to face a tall woman, drop-dead gorgeous, perhaps twenty years older than he was, maybe more. Briefly, his eyes took it all in—the platinum hair, no doubt dyed for effect, the designer pantsuit and stiletto heels, the expensive jewelry, sunglasses, the ample cleavage showing through the V-neckline. The woman could easily have been a movie star. *Face job, probably; boob job, too.* "I-I'm going to Orlando," he said, adding out of courtesy, "how about you?"

The woman tilted her sunglasses up with a hairband effect, revealing unusual violet eyes fringed by thick black lashes. "Orlando as well," she said with a throaty chuckle. She held out her boarding pass, obviously wanting to compare it with his. He flashed his. "Well, what do you know?"

Eric smiled. "Looks like we're sitting together." He cleared his throat. "My wife won't be joining me until Christmas," he said. "Are you married too?" The last thing he wanted to do was give the wrong impression. He didn't usually enjoy chitchat, but he also didn't want to pass the entire flight in awkward silence.

"I'm Erika with a K," she said with a toothy smile. "Not currently married. Maybe one of these days, I'll try it again. For the time being, I'm free as a bird… the line's moving."

As he caught up in line, he said over his shoulder, "My name's Eric with a C, by the way."

"We are just one coincidence after another, aren't we, darling?"

Can you say "cougar"? It was Eric's turn to show his ID and boarding pass to the TSA agent. As he put his shoes back on, Erika sat down beside him and wriggled her feet into her high heels.

"As soon as we're on the plane, these babies are coming off again," she purred.

Eric was not accustomed to being flirted with; he certainly didn't want to flirt back. Just then, he felt the vibration of his phone in his pocket. "Excuse me," he said and pulled his carry-on with him to a more private space to answer the call.

"I am miserable already," Donna said. From the background noise, Eric could tell she was at the office. "How will I *survive* until Christmas?"

"I miss you too, babe," he said. They talked about the drive with Chet and about Donna's plans to eat at the Hendersons' for Thanksgiving.

"I know you've got to go, babe," Donna said. "I hope you have someone interesting to talk to on the plane."

Eric cleared his throat. "Actually, I've already met her."

Silence, then, "And?"

Eric laughed out loud, causing a few passers-by to turn their heads. "And she's twenty years older than I am, and I love my wife." *No need to tell her what she looks like or seems to be interested in.*

Donna giggled at the other end. Eric could picture her in his mind, so bubbly and blonde—so different from the way she acted as soon as she entered the red room as his Domme. He sat down in a nearby seat to cover his excitement. *Odd. I never felt like this with Jessica. Just* thinking *about Donna does it, just hearing her voice.*

"I'm glad she's older," Donna said. "I want you to have a good time, but I'm definitely okay with you not traveling to Florida with some twenty-something who wants to join the Mile-High Club."

"What's the Mile-High Club?"

"You are adorable, you know that?" Donna explained what she'd assumed anyone their age knew: The Mile-High Club was slang for people who had sex aboard an airplane.

Judging from the vibes he'd picked up from Erika, that was probably well within the realm of possibility despite the age difference. No need to mention it, however. Eric spoke quietly so that no one around him could hear. "The only woman I want to have sex with is my wife," he said. "Any—"

Donna chimed in to complete the phrase with him. "Time. Any place. Any way. Only you. " It was their private mantra.

A crisp voice over the airport's intercom interrupted the call. When the message ended, Eric said goodbye. "I'll call you tonight, babe. Love you!"

As he walked to his gate, he saw that Erika was seated beside a distinguished looking gentleman, engaged in an animated conversation. *She really is attractive*, Eric thought. And they made an attractive couple. *Better you than me, buddy. Better you than me.*

When they got on the plane, however, Erika was obviously thrilled to see him again. She pointed to her naked, pedicured feet. "See? I told you. Have to let the toes breathe now and then."

Before Eric could comment, the gentleman from the waiting area made his presence known in the aisle beside them with a little grunt. "Excuse me," he said in an accented baritone. "I say, chap, would you mind switching seats with me so that the lady and I could continue our conversation?"

Eric looked at Erika, whose face was unreadable, at least to him. She bit her glossy red lips as her eyes moved past Eric to the other man. Eric took that as a signal. "Of course not, sir," he said, rising from the aisle seat. "Where's your seat?"

A few minutes later, Eric settled back into the window seat. There was no one beside him, which was what he preferred. He hadn't flown often, never in first class, but this boded well for the whole Florida experience. Peace and quiet. He'd nap a little, maybe dream of that fantastic night at the club. *The Mile-High Club has nothing on my Donna,* he thought, drifting off.

Donna walked to the photography room. Paul and Lance were engrossed in work at their computers and didn't hear her come in. "Gentlemen?" she said.

Both swiveled their chairs around. "Who's spreading *that* rumor?" Lance sneered.

Ignoring the comment, she addressed Paul, "Those close-ups you took for me? Worth asked if you could zoom out on the one of the mayor and get more of the crowd that was there?"

"Sure thing, Donnala," Paul said.

Donna glanced at Lance then left the room. In a moment, he was at her elbow. "Donnala?" he murmured. "I think I'd rather call you Donna*let*. As in 'Donna lets' me take her out some time."

Donna stopped. Lance stopped. Donna looked around, wishing they were in a less public spot in the building, but come to think of it, that was probably a good thing. A little louder than necessary, she said, "Perhaps you didn't realize, but I got married a few days ago." She held her left hand up to make the point, waving it so her rings were unmistakable. "So, no, I will not *let* you do anything at all, other than conduct yourself professionally around me."

A few of the people seated close by snickered. Donna didn't like the way Lance's expression changed—it wasn't embarrassment. Something akin to rage flickered in his eyes, but only for a second.

Lance's eyes returned to normal as he bowed with a flourish. "My apology, madame. I meant it as a joke. No need to get your knickers in a twist." He turned to speak to one of the men who had overheard,

Probably something vile and off-color, Donna assumed as she walked back to her cubicle. *I can't let him get to me. Oh, Eric, I wish you were here.*

The Steins' house was enormous. "Okina Mizu—Big Waters, roughly, in Japanese," Ari Stein explained as he gave Eric an abbreviated grand tour. "I spent many happy years in Japan in my youth, so you'll notice the influence here and there. Some areas of the house were off-limits to servants, he said. "Not that you're a servant, per se, but we do ask you to respect our boundaries."

"Of course, Mr. Stein," Eric said. After the flight and the drive—*pleasant company, that chauffeur*—he was anxious to see the layout of the room where he would construct the fireplace.

Big Waters was so named because it sat on a narrow section of barrier island just north of Vero Beach. West windows on the second and third floors had a beautiful view of the sparkling Indian River, while windows on the east side of the mansion faced the Atlantic. In the distance, Eric spotted high rise condominiums but here, surrounded by landscaping and pine trees, no other home was in view. Traffic from the road that connected them to Vero, as well as north to Cape Canaveral, was barely audible within the lush confines of the estate.

"We value our privacy," Ari was saying as they walked. "We throw parties quite often, but otherwise, we're homebodies. Everything we need and want is brought in. Well, here it is."

Photographs had been sent by text and email, but nothing had prepared him for the sheer size of the job. Because of the time crunch before New Year's, he had encouraged them to order the stone and other materials to arrive before he did. Field stone from Italy, along with everything on his list, was there waiting.

The room itself was huge. Floor to ceiling glass on two sides of a vast wall revealed the private beach access with privacy walls ending about fifty yards from the water. There was a bar to the right as they entered, a conversation pit to one side. Centered on the focus wall was a large electric fireplace.

The room appeared to be new, with expensive, ornate molding around the ceiling and baseboard. The walls were painted a light tan, accenting the polished parquet floor. When the stonework was complete, it would be magnificent.

Anticipating Eric's question, Ari beamed. "Yes, this is new construction. We'd only been here a few months when Doris—you'll meet her this evening—said we must expand. There simply wasn't enough 'party room' as she called it. And you'll see what she means next week. We're having a Thanksgiving 'do', and she's invited the whole of our usual party group. The society we belong to looks forward to it every year, but along the way, we have gatherings at other locations as well as here."

Eric nodded, not really paying attention. Mentally, he was measuring the area and writing another materials list. He'd need more scaffolding than he'd anticipated, in order to reach the top section and more drop cloths and padding to protect the parquet. Doris Stein had wanted imported fieldstone to remind her of her childhood summers in Italy, but it would have been better to postpone the flooring until after it was laid. No matter, it would just be more expense. And it was evident that expense was not a factor for the Steins in any way.

Everywhere Eric looked, he saw only the finest quality fixtures and furnishings. The home was modern, a 'smart home', with advanced technology discreetly in place. Despite mention of servants, Eric had met the friendly chauffeur, who had picked him up in Orlando, and the diminutive cook, who had brought out a tray of snacks upon his arrival. Both had been personable, Asian of some variety, but not overly curious about him. Apparently, they were the resident staff, with day workers for the elaborate landscaping, pool maintenance, and other jobs.

"You have *carte blanche* while you're here, Eric," Ari was saying. "Anything you need to make your stay more comfort-able. The passwords to all the 'gadgets', as Doris calls them, are on a list in your room, plus other materials that will better explain our home and atmosphere. You have a suite, with a private living area and bathroom I think your wife will enjoy during her visit. I'm not going to check on you much, trusting you to know what you're doing and how long it will take. Feel free to enjoy the pool, the gym, the beach, the Jacuzzi, the kitchen—any door that isn't locked is yours to explore, as long as you get the fireplace done by December thirtieth, so Doris can have her grand opening party for New Year's. That's all she's talked about for months now." He chuckled.

"Oh, and by the way," he continued, "we're flying to Italy for Christmas, so you and your wife will have the place virtually to yourselves. We operate with a skeleton staff only, but I give them several weeks off for the holidays. Usually, I have someone come in for security, but I'm sure you and your wife will be enough to ward off any interlopers." He laughed. "Seriously, unless you know we're here, you'd never know from the road, would you?"

Eric had to agree. When the Town Car had pulled in, it had felt like they were headed into a dense pine forest. Only when they stopped so that the chauffeur could enter the gate code, did it appear they were, in fact, approaching civilization. *Donna's going to love this place. And with utter privacy, I'll tell her to bring some "toys" for sure.* He'd just arrived in Florida, and already, he could hardly wait for her to come. His cheeks reddened. *Come indeed.*

Eric worked every day from six until six, pausing only when Asahi, the cook, brought him refreshments. She reminded him of a tiny doll—a rather ordinary doll—but her culinary skills were a wonder, based on the foods she delivered several times a day. She was comfortable enough around him now that she would sit and chat a bit as he ate at the bar or in the conversation pit, away from his tools and materials. He was careful to protect all the surfaces from his dust.

It had only taken a few days of solitude for Eric to engage Asahi in conversation. The Steins rarely made an appearance, and other than those precious FaceTime calls each night with Donna, Eric was getting lonely.

"What does your name mean?" he asked one afternoon as he set his bowl of miso soup down on the bar.

Asahi lowered her head shyly. "It is Japanese, for morning sunshine."

Eric smiled. "That's lovely. And appropriate, Asahi. You bring sunshine every time you bring me food. This place is awfully quiet."

"You should play music, Eric-san," she said with a little bow. "Just tell the house."

"Tell the house?"

Asahi giggled, covering her mouth. "I put instructions in your room. Set it up to obey your voice, and then wherever you are, you tell the house what you want to hear. Like this." Asahi looked up and spoke more loudly. "I want to hear J-pop," she announced to the air.

Instantly, guitar music and Japanese lyrics wafted through the big room from several directions. "My favorite group," she said.

I'll need to set it up for myself, definitely, thought Eric. Music would help pass the time, but he decided that after a few hours of J-pop, he'd be hungering for something in English. "Nice. Thanks, I'll work on it. So tell me about this Thanksgiving party," Eric said, standing. He brushed his hands off before he gloved up again for work.

Asahi giggled again, her eyes wide. "Ooh. Are you going to the party, Eric-san? I make all of the food but will have the night off."

Eric was offended on her behalf. He turned to her with a frown. "They don't let you go, after you did all the work? That's not right."

Asahi shook her head, her eyes bright. "Oh no, Eric-san. I do not *want* to go to the party. *Pochapocha.*" She laughed. "But you—you would be fine, Eric-san."

"*Pochapocha?*"

Asahi laughed as she left him with a wave. "*Pochapocha, pochapocha.*"

I'll have to google that. Eric took a deep breath. *Four more hours of work. Steam shower in the gym. The dinner Asahi will have left in my room, and then Donna.* She had a way of making their FaceTime calls quite the adventure.

7

An Early Celebration

"Everything was delicious," Worth commented as the family festivities wound down at the Hendersons'. Because Worth's mother was popping in for a quick visit on Thursday, everyone had agreed to move their celebration to Wednesday instead. No one at the magazine had minded getting an extra day off, and the schools at which Keith and Jon taught had taken the entire week for Thanksgiving break. Layla had given her notice when she started experiencing discomfort, but Kari still worked as a paralegal.

Layla groaned, rubbing her belly. Now in the second trimester of her pregnancy, she could legitimately wear maternity clothes. Before, she'd gotten away with fuller lines and larger sizes, but there was no mistaking the baby bump at this point. "I know I'm eating for two, but today, I think I must've eaten for four or five."

Keith put his arm around her. "This is no time to diet, sweetheart." He kissed the top of her head.

Jessica nodded. "Enjoy it while you can. Mom keeps telling me that at a certain age, we'll all wish we had exercised more."

Across the long table, Carol laughed. "Well, it's true." She stood to fetch a pitcher of iced tea for refills, her hands on her hips. "I have to really work to keep this figure."

Chet beamed proudly. "I heartily approve."

It was a full house—Chet and Carol, Jessica and Worth, Chet's daughter Kari and her husband Jon, Chet's son Keith and his wife Layla, and Donna. And it also was, Donna thought, the happiest Thanksgiving she'd had in many years, even with Eric out of state. "Thank you again for having me," she said. "I really appreciate it."

"But of course!" Chet boomed. "What do you hear from the stonemason?"

Donna smiled, remembering last night's FaceTime. She'd dressed up as a sexy police officer for him, tantalizing him by holding her phone at various angles so he could see every inch of skin that showed through the outfit. *Thank heaven for overnight delivery.* She'd get an idea at work, place the order, and look forward to surprising Eric soon.

"He's all settled in at this grand estate right on the ocean," she said. "It sounds heavenly. I can't wait to visit next month."

When Worth put on his editor "hat" to ask if she'd put in the paperwork for the time off, Jessica punched him lightly. "What? I like to keep up with things," he said with a laugh.

"Yes, boss," Donna said with a giggle. "I submitted the paperwork to Skip, boss, just like you said, boss."

Worth threw up his hands in mock defeat. "Okay, okay. This is a holiday. Sorry." Since he and Jessica had gotten married, her role at the magazine had increased. She still wrote features and a monthly 'back page' column, but he was steadily teaching her the business side of things. Soon, perhaps Skip would be assistant to both of them.

Layla interrupted with a little groan. "What is it, hon?" Keith asked.

"Oh, nothing. Just indigestion from all that great food, I'm sure," she said, rising from her seat. "I just need to go to the——" Her eyes widened in fear. "No! It's too soon!"

The unmistakable sound of water dripping onto the tile floor brought gasps from everyone else. Carol had just come in. "Call 9-1-1. Layla, lie down *stat*."

Donna was surprised by the authority in Carol's voice, then she remembered that she had been a nurse before Jessica was born, and again after Jessica started school. That's how she'd met Jessica's father, in fact. Today, having a nurse around was fortuitous. Everyone's face was drawn with concern.

"Jess," Donna said quietly as they tensely waited for the ambulance to arrive, "I'll clean up here, so you can all go to the hospital, and lock up before I leave."

Jessica nodded. "Thanks," she said, squeezing her friend's hand. "I don't know what she'd do if …" Her voice trailed off.

Donna laid her head on Jessica's shoulder. Everything and everyone she could think of at the moment paled in comparison. Deadlines, that jerk at work, the Peeping Tom reports, Eric, the club. Nothing mattered right now but Layla and the baby.

Inspired by those events, Donna had ordered a sexy nurse's outfit. What material there was, was crisp white, edged in red, with red straps crisscrossing her back and sides. White thigh-high stockings were also edged in red lace. Atop her blonde curls, sat a little white nurse's cap with a red cross. "What do you think? Are you in need of some *oral* medication?" she asked Eric seductively on the video call.

In Florida, Eric rolled his eyes in approval. "Oh my lord, Donna," he said huskily. "You really know how to make it hard on a guy."

"Hard already, big guy?" Donna teased. "I wish I could give you mouth-to-mouth resuscitation."

"I miss you. So. Much." Eric waited while Donna repositioned her phone so that he could see her from the back. She bent over and began pumping her knees, wiggling her tiny butt in the air, looking around to make kiss lips at the screen.

"Do you like this angle, doctor? Or are you my patient? How about you show me what effect I'm having. This video goes both ways, you know."

Normally, Eric would have been embarrassed to show himself. He felt self-conscious about the size of his penis "at rest" so to speak. Fueled by the sight of Donna's costume, however, his manhood was suitably engorged for her inspection. "Hold on." He put down the phone so that he could unzip his jeans and drop them to the floor along with his plaid boxers. A little chagrined, he picked the phone up and held it below his waist.

"Oh, babe, I would love to be holding on to that," Donna said breathlessly. Suddenly, she was stern. "Now I want you to do it. I will too."

"What?" Eric had never been much for self-pleasuring. He knew other guys did it regularly, but he had never felt the need.

Donna brought the phone up to her mouth and licked her lips provocatively. "You don't want me to diagnose blue balls, do you, lover?"

"I've just never... you know, in front of someone."

Donna giggled as she brought the phone down where she was in full view again. "And you think I have, mister? The sight of that... enormous... cock just turned me on so much, I thought maybe we could try. Please?" she pouted before flashing a grin.

Eric agreed. She'd talked him through that first night in the red room. Maybe she'd talk him through this. In Florida, he lay on the plush bed in his suite.

Back home, Donna unsnapped the crotch of her costume and lay down on their bed. "Just watch me for now," she purred. Setting up the phone so that he could see her torso, Donna pulled her breasts from the scraps of material holding them and began to squeeze her nipples, making soft noises of pleasure as she did.

Instinctively, Eric's hands went to his lap. Although he wore gloves while he worked, his hands were dry and scratchy. Reaching for a bottle thoughtfully left for guests on the nightstand, he massaged his hands with the fragrant lotion and tried again. "That's better," he murmured, encircling his member with both thumbs and middle fingers, gripping himself tightly as he moved his hands up and down, his eyes never leaving his wife's image.

Donna walked her hands slowly down her sides, playing with the red ribbons along her ribs and hips, pulling the material up from between her legs to expose the blonde triangle. When she'd asked Eric about getting a Brazilian wax, he had been adamant. "If you look like a little girl down there," he'd told her, pointing to his crotch, "I don't think I'd have the desired response *here.*"

Now Donna moved the phone so that he could see her legs spread wide on the bed. "I wish this was your tongue and not my fingers," she said, "but we'll just have to make do."

As she fingered her labia, played with the curls, and gently stroked her clit, Donna's hips began to rock. In concert with her movements, Eric adjusted the speed of his hands. He closed his eyes and imagined them together. Faster, faster, harder, harder... and there! Hot ejaculate sprayed his chest and he dropped the phone to the side, spent for the moment.

He could hear Donna's moans coming from the phone and picked it up again. In her excitement, she had forgotten the phone altogether, but it had landed where he could see her face, albeit at a strange angle. He watched her face contort in pleasure as she cried out.

Donna's whole body shuddered, and she lay still and quiet, neither knowing nor caring at the moment if he was watching or still connected or anything other than the incredibly empowering feeling that swept through her. *I don't need a man for this.* Immediately, that thought was followed by *but I want one.* It was a revelation.

A few seconds passed. Then another few seconds. Making soft noises, Donna picked the phone up again and was pleased to see Eric's face on the screen. Both of them were still breathing a bit more heavily than normal. "That was… good, right?"

Eric smirked a little. "Oh, *hell* yeah. Spectacular. Babe, you are always teaching me something new."

Donna frowned a little. "Perhaps it's your turn to teach *me* something new."

When Eric made no reply, she continued, "Just don't think I'm going to go this easy on you when I'm there in person. This was a more-than-decent substitute because of the distance, but—"

"Goes without saying, Donna," Eric whispered. He looked down at his chest. "Whew. I'm a bit of a mess. Hold on while I clean up?"

"That's okay," Donna said as she yawned. "Wait until after the party tomorrow to call. I want to hear all about it."

Eric gave himself the whole day off. He tidied up his work area in case any guests wanted to see his progress, sunned on the beach, and lifted weights in the home gym. He also teased Asahi in the kitchen as she cooked for the party.

"I googled *pochapocha*," he said, pouring himself a glass of fresh lemonade. She'd made the pitcher with lemons from the estate, sweetening it with local honey. "It means pudgy. I don't get it. One, you're not pudgy, and two, why would it matter if you were?"

Asahi paused as she kneaded the dough for yeast rolls on the butcher-block island. "Thank you, Eric-san. *I* think I am too pudgy for the Steins' party and besides, I-I am driving to Vero to see a movie with a friend." She smiled mischievously. "I think that you should definitely go, though."

"Friend? Asahi has a boyfriend," he sang until she shook her head.

"Her name is Nancy."

"Nancy, Nancy. So is this party fancy-shmancy? I mostly brought work clothes and swim trunks."

Asahi giggled again as she kneaded the dough. "Party will be *very* casual. More than you'd think."

What does that even mean? Before he could ask, a familiar face popped up over the saloon door.

"Eric with a C!" Erika-with-a-K cooed. "I didn't know you were coming to the Steins. I could have given you a lift from the airport." Erika pushed the doors open, ignoring Asahi completely as she walked over to Eric. She stood closer than he would have preferred, her hips cocked and the improbable chest jutting forward in invitation.

Eric looked at Asahi for back-up, but her expression clearly communicated that Eric-san was on his own. Perhaps Erika was a regular visitor? "I, um, a ride was already arranged. Maybe if we'd sat together on the plane, it would have come up in conversation but—"

Erika made a face as she picked up a piece of celery on the butcher-block and took a bite. "Oh, *him*. I invited him to the party, but we'll see. A bit of a prude, I think. Anyway, I arrived early because I want to get some sun before tonight. It's been so dreadfully cold up north, I am white as a ghost. Don't want to scare anyone off." She laughed.

There seemed to be something going on that Eric couldn't quite put a finger on. *Casual party, Asahi's deliberately vague or going on about being* pochapocha, *Erika's worried about her tan.* It didn't add up.

"Would you like to see my progress?" Party forgotten for the moment, Eric wanted to show off his handiwork. Asahi always commented, and the Steins had been in now and then, but things were really shaping up. He had a long way to go, but you could tell now that the fireplace would be magnificent when finished.

"Indeed! When you said you were putting in a fireplace, I was thinking a *regular* fireplace. If I'd known you were the kind of craftsman up to Ari and *Doris's standards,* there's no way I would have let that man switch seats with you. You *must* be something special."

Eric pointed in the general direction of the addition and followed Erika out, but not before he distinctly heard Asahi say quietly, "Careful, Eric-san. Be very careful."

8

Thanksgiving Party

D oris Stein was a vivacious redhead, pleasingly *pochapocha* in Eric's opinion. She and Ari were both on the short side, but comfortable both financially and relationally. Eric didn't see them often, but they'd made favorable impressions on one another. "I'm delighted you're coming to the party," Doris told him by intercom. "Asahi explained everything? My friend Erika, I believe you already met. Everyone else should be here by six. It's quite a group. And they'll be everywhere—beach, pool, Jacuzzi. Probably not the gym. Living room, all around. I just didn't want you to walk anywhere and be surprised."

Asahi explained nada, he thought but said nothing. He waited until six-thirty to make his way downstairs. Ari and Doris inhabited the north wing, which they kept locked at all times. His room and the other guest rooms were on the third floor of the south wing. The chauffeur and Asahi were housed on the second floor, south, with rooms for others as needed. It had seemed odd to him, at first, to have an elevator in a house, but at the end of a long day of laying stone, he was thankful for it.

Eric checked his reflection in the mirror. He was wearing

his hair long tonight—it was Florida, right? He'd carefully ironed the one Hawaiian shirt he'd packed. He wore khaki shorts and leather flip-flops he'd picked up at the airport. His beard was neatly trimmed. He nodded with appreciation. Hard work, breaks on the beach, and Asahi's cooking had made a difference. His hair was bleached lighter by the sun. His skin was bronzed, his muscles ripped. *Donna will approve.* She'd commented on his hair and tan, of course, but he was looking forward to showing her the whole *package* in a few weeks.

The elevator was in use, so Eric walked down the modern, winding staircase. As he neared the bottom, he heard voices coming toward him. Doris, Ari, and Erika breezed into view carrying cocktails. At the sight of them, Eric froze. They were completely nude.

"*There* you are," Erika called up to him. "Just finishing work? Go get changed and join us."

Without answering her, Eric turned on his heel and bounded up the stairs, stopping at the second floor. He walked down the hallway and called quietly for Asahi. When she opened her door and saw his face, her hands flew to her face to cover her laughter.

"You brat!" he said. "Why didn't you tell me?"

Asahi shook her head. "Oh, Eric-san. This will teach you to read instructions. Along with the passwords, was a pamphlet for the local naturists' society, which meets here every month. Tonight, in fact. You just didn't bother to read it."

"You mean everyone at the party is naked?"

Asahi nodded. "They aren't swingers if that's what you're thinking. Naturists enjoy being free from clothing. The Steins keep their wing locked for that reason, although when there are no… textile… guests, they wander the whole estate like that. It took a bit of getting used it."

"Textile?"

"You're a textile. I'm a textile. We prefer to wear clothes.

But maybe not tonight, Eric-san?" Her eyes were bright with amusement.

Eric sighed. The Steins had gone to great expense to bring him to their home. Doris had been excited when he agreed to join the party. It wasn't their fault he hadn't read the pamphlet. He didn't want to be uncourteous, but he was concerned. What if he got excited? His brain replied with a visual of Doris, Erika, and Ari; perhaps that *wouldn't* be a problem. But what if all the guys were... bigger? It was a deep-seated fear. *What would Donna want me to do?*

In his mind, he saw Donna in dominatrix glory, admonishing him sternly. Eric threw up his hands and said, "'When in Rome!'"

Asahi gave him a little bow. "In Japan, we say, 'When you enter a village, obey the village.' Goodnight—off to meet Nancy now."

Eric pivoted as he waved goodbye and headed for his suite, throwing his clothes on the bed. He stood in front of the full-length mirror for almost a minute, shaking his head, grimacing at his tan lines. His white genitals and buttocks would certainly identify him as a textile, unfamiliar with the naturist lifestyle. "I'm younger than most, anyway." With a sigh, he headed back downstairs.

Erika was the first person he encountered. He instantly congratulated himself on his assumption at the airport—no way a woman her age had natural breasts *that* perky. She wore a long pendant to draw eyes there and noticed her success with Eric. "They cost a bundle, darling, but everyone says they're worth it." She stepped closer. "Want to see how real they feel?" She laughed at his expression and pulled him by his bicep. "Ooh la la. Come on; let's go."

As they walked into the living room, Eric blinked at the sea of skin. Nowhere did he spot the least bit of self-consciousness or lust, however. Ari brought him a glass filled with rich amber liquid.

Eric thanked him and took a sip, coughing a little. The taste of peat was strong, but it was incredibly smooth. *Expensive. Of course.*

"Talisker can bring you to your knees," Ari said. "Be aware." He leaned up to whisper in Eric's ear. "Also watch out for Erika. She's a bit wilder than the rest of our little group."

Eric nodded without comment, taking another, smaller sip.

Erika pulled at his arm. "I want to introduce you to someone." She pulled him along with her, leaving the living room and stepping outside, where a woman about her age was sipping a drink as she dangled her legs in the pool. "Jillian! I want you to meet someone."

At her name, the woman turned. Her straight hair was cut very short. Slimmer than Erika, her shape was more like Donna's than Jessica's. Her face was more natural, too, more appealing to Eric than Erika's movie star glamour. *No plastic surgery there,* Eric surmised.

Seeing him, Jillian gave her friend a nod. "I'll bet I know what you have in mind for this fine stud."

Eric frowned. He wasn't used to female attention other than from Donna. Now that he had it in spades, he realized that attention from these two, beautiful as they were, made him uncomfortable.

"Let's sit, shall we?" Erika cooed.

Eric sat beside Jillian, appreciating the cool water on his feet. Florida was having an unusually hot autumn and the night air was still warm. Erika took a seat on the other side of Eric and inched over until her hips just barely touched his.

"I don't want to shock you, Eric," she began quietly, "but Ari and Doris's parties can be a bit dull. I enjoy visiting so I can catch up with Doris—we went to college together, you know—

but I always try to find a way to make the trip more... memorable. *Capisce?*"

Eric did not *capisce*. A first-class trip to a Florida estate for a party of naturists seemed entirely memorable just as it was. The cautions Asahi and Ari had offered sprang to mind; his heart began to pound.

Erika laid a manicured hand on Eric's thigh, making his cock jump a little. "Oh, but abso*lute*ly are you going to make this worthwhile, lover." She paused, looking across the pool. If anyone noticed them, they would see three party-goers enjoying light conversation as they kicked at the water. Nothing unseemly.

Jillian took a sip of her drink. "What Erika means is that this is your lucky night too. We have a proposal for you. We do the party, the small talk, the food, for an acceptable amount of time..."

Erika continued, "And then we retire to your suite for the *real* party."

Eric was appalled. "Both of you?"

Erika threw her head back with delight. "Of *course*, both of us." She looked directly at Eric. "A threesome. You, Jillian, me. We do each other. We do you." She gave a little wave of her hand. "Whatever combination comes to mind."

Eric slipped into the water to face them, trying to hide his distaste. They were attractive, there was no doubt about it, but they could both be his mothers! And he was married! "Ladies," he said gently but firmly, "thanks for the invitation, but no. If you'll excuse me, Ari wanted me to show some folks the fireplace."

He walked through the water to the steps and got out, grabbing the towel Doris had brought him and drying himself before he headed back inside. As he did, he could hear Erika grousing in bits and pieces. "Damn him... flirted..."

Jillian's comment made him chuckle: "That one's strung

too tightly, Erika. If he's got a sex life, it must be vanilla as all get out."

Donna was breathless with giggles. "I'm sorry, Eric. I know it's not really funny, but the thought of you walking into a room of geezers with no clothes on. That is hilarious."

Eric joined her laughter. "It was unique; that's for sure! But you know what? After about a minute, I hardly noticed. Everyone carries a towel, which I, of course, didn't know, but Doris got one for me. You put the towel wherever you sit, for courtesy and hygiene. They don't give it a second thought, so neither did I, after the initial shock. And they were all so *nice.*"

"Be honest—were they all old, or were there some babes there too?"

"There were... younger people there, yes. A few couples brought their grown children. There were even a few *younger* children—grandkids."

Donna was amazed. "Wow. So it really isn't about sex, then."

"Not at all. Just a lifestyle. The people I talked to said they're naturists at home. Some of them live at a naturist resort about an hour away. They get together socially at least once a month, bowling, pot-lucks, things any group might do, just without clothes. There's a nude beach a bit south of here that they love and maintain, but the Steins also let the group use their beach access here."

Eric thought it prudent to *not* mention his embarrassing sofa pillow incident. When the first rather striking young mother had walked across the room holding her toddler by the hand, nature had kicked in unexpectedly. He'd gotten acclimated to the older bodies wandering in and out of the room, but she was the type who turns heads on the sidewalk. Fortunately, a pillow was close enough to grab and place discreetly on his lap.

"No worries," a man sitting close by had encouraged quietly. "Always a bit of a challenge at first for new guys your age. For us? Not so much." He'd smiled at his friend beside him, pointing to his toupee. "We notice up here, of course."

He'd noticed something surprisingly comforting, though, that he *did* mention to Donna. He couldn't help but see the roomfuls of genitals; they were just *there*. He was actually more interested in *that* aspect than multitude of breasts showing various degrees of gravity. He'd read that in the flaccid state, penises were fairly uniform in size, but he'd never believed it. He certainly hadn't researched it himself.

"Not that I studied every man's junk, but I can say with some authority now that all men *are* created equal in some respects," Eric told Donna. When she giggled, he went on. "In *some* respects. Penises, about the same regardless of age or race, just hanging there in limbo. Balls? Now that's another story." Dimensions had ranged from ping-pong balls to softballs.

When he told her about the threesome invite, she was appropriately livid. "The nerve of those biddies!"

Apparently, the mental picture Donna had conjured differed significantly from reality, but he didn't contradict her. If she drew comfort from thinking a couple of dowdy grandmas had tried to chat him up, that was fine.

"It was flattering, actually," he said.

"Hm. Well, I understand—even the jerk at work who annoys me—I mean, he noticed. That's something," Donna agreed.

"Jerk?"

"I mentioned the new photographer to you earlier, didn't I?" Donna asked.

Donna had been upset all out of proportion, in his opinion.

"He's harmless, I'm sure," Eric said. "Just a guy being a guy. Hey, any more problems with the Peeping Toms?"

There had been additional reports scattered throughout the city, and women were on edge. Jessica was working on a column about self-defense training, Donna explained. "Anything to give them more peace of mind."

Donna and Eric talked the longest they'd talked since he left, getting updates on their respective jobs, what was going on with Layla and the baby, Donna's part-time work at the club, a bit of trouble with that hadn't amounted to anything.

"Trouble? What kind of trouble?"

"My second night on the job and I thought I'd lost my keys! And then the next day, they were in my purse. Sheesh. I thought I was losing it," Donna chirped. "I mean, I know what they say about blondes, but that's the first time I felt like such a ditz."

Before saying goodnight, they spoke of Christmas plans. Donna was excited to learn that they'd have the estate practically to themselves. "That says a lot about you, babe. They *trust* you. I can hardly wait to start packing!"

Eric laughed. "I'll be working, remember. We'll be stuck there at the house, pretty much. Pack light, I'm saying. Very light. Extremely light. Light, as in an empty bag, light like—"

"I got the idea, *Eric-san*," Donna teased. "I wish Asahi was going to be there. She sounds like someone I'd like to meet."

9

The Ten-Cent Tour

C arol Henderson brought a tray into her new stepdaughter-in-law's room. "Ready for lunch, I hope?"

Layla sighed. "You are so good to me, Carol. Thanks for staying. I trust Pops is managing okay?" She sat up straighter and adjusted the pillows behind her so that she could eat in bed. After her water had broken the day before Thanksgiving, her doctor had put her on complete bed rest.

Layla settled the tray of soup and sandwich in front of her belly as Carol sat beside the bed in a nearby chair. "Chet's fine. He wants to spend this weekend here, though, if that's okay with you and Keith."

"Of course! Mm, this smells delicious. Nothing beats homemade chicken soup," Layla said.

Carol laughed. "Sorry to disappoint you, but it's from a can." Carol was still getting used to the various personalities in her new extended family but was determined to do all she could to foster good relationships. Not only was it important to her, it was important to Chet. "I'm glad we can give Chet a good report." A visiting nurse practitioner had checked on Layla that morning.

Layla nodded as she finished a bite of sandwich. "I feel kind of foolish, though. When we met you in the summer, I thought I was barely pregnant. Good thing I was further along than that."

"Absolutely. But first babies have a way of surprising us. I'm so thankful your little bunch of broccoli is bigger than you thought, or…" Carol stopped. Layla was in her seventh month, not her fourth as she'd mistakenly thought. A premature rupture of the membranes that early would have been disastrous. As it was, the doctor had put her on bed rest, antibiotics, and a round of steroids to help the baby's lungs develop, in case of a premature delivery. And the baby *was* about the size of a bunch of broccoli by now.

Tears welled up in Layla's eyes. "I was so scared I'd lose it. Her. Him." She smiled and patted her belly. "If you hadn't been with me, I might not have gone to the hospital as fast. Thank you so much."

Carol stood up. "You'll be just fine, dear. I'm going to tidy up. I'll call Chet and let him know he can come over. When Keith comes home from school, maybe I'll order pizza. How does that sound?"

Layla giggled. "That sounds great. Oh! I completely forgot when the NP came. My little sister called. She's coming during her Christmas break so she can take over nurse duties. You'll be off the hook."

"Kristina, right?" Carol hadn't met Layla's sister yet but had spoken to her a few times on the phone. Quiet, almost timid, just a year or two younger than Layla, she was a teacher at the school Keith had worked at before they moved. Something in the ESE department, autistic children, she thought. Carol smiled and closed the bedroom door behind herself. This was good news—this weekend, and then a break coming soon. She and Chet had only been married a few months, after all.

Carol whistled a tune as she walked to the kitchen, speaking to the fat calico cat as she passed it, "You know, we new brides don't like to sleep alone, no matter what our age."

In response, the cat followed her into the kitchen, hoping for a treat.

Jessica had to stop eating as she listened to Donna's animated recap of Eric's Thanksgiving experience; she'd almost choked on a bite of taco salad, she was laughing so hard. The fact that Eric had even agreed to a rather public appearance in the nude was proof he had changed drastically since they'd been a couple.

She'd nodded appreciatively at the photo of "Florida Eric". His hair had always been his one vanity, but it looked even better now, sun-bleached, below his shoulders. *He looks like a Greek god.* And nude? No wonder those old ladies had fawned all over him. *Not that he looks better than Worth*, she thought quickly.

Worth had to travel, but she had opted to stay home in case her mom needed help with Layla. Then Chet called to say *he* was spending the weekend there. Jessica was in a funk. A wasted weekend without Worth… sometimes she could hardly believe how happy they were, how perfectly matched they were.

"He'll finish the fireplace while I'm there," Donna was saying, "but I'm sure he won't get as much done with me hanging all over him. I mean, we had like three days after the wedding? I *really* miss him."

The hunger in her eyes made Jessica chuckle. "Well, it sounds like you're making the most of Face Timing." Donna had shown her some of the outfits she'd bought for the occasion. Eric had been so enthusiastic, apparently, that she'd asked Worth about it. Would he like her to order anything?

'Nothing doing,' he'd told her. 'When I get tired of seeing you naked, I'll buy you something. Until then, I want skin, skin, and more skin.' Her cheeks colored at the thought. Last night's "goodbye sex" had been quite memorable.

"Uh oh," Donna suddenly said, staring across the restaurant.

"What? What's wrong?" Jessica followed Donna's eye, grazing the room until she spotted a familiar face. Lance Glover was in a booth, eating alone. "Oh, did you want to ask him to join us?" she teased. Personally, she had no opinion of the man one way or the other, but she was well aware of Donna's dislike.

Donna attacked her chimichanga in response. "Like that will ever happen. He's creepy. Sometimes I think he follows me. He sure does pop up frequently."

Jessica smirked. "The office isn't that big, Donna. And people do eat lunch. He wanted Mexican today, and so did we. That's all."

"I guess," Donna said with a grimace. "I don't know what it is about him that gets to me—I mean he says things, or did, until I told him off in front of everybody. Now he just *looks* creepy. Stares." She glanced over at him and caught his eye. "Like now."

When Jessica glanced over, however, he was eating. "What?"

"Never mind. Maybe I'm on edge because Eric's gone. He says it's nothing to worry about too."

The two finished, paid their bills, and chatted happily as they walked back to work. Neither of them had much planned for the weekend, other than a yoga class for Jessica and a determination to sleep late for Donna. They decided to catch a movie the next evening. "I'm working a few hours in the afternoon, though," Donna said.

"Right, your part-time gig," Jessica said. "I could pick you up there, if you want."

Donna grinned. *Won't* you *be surprised!* "Sure! Come at six, and I'll give you the ten-cent tour."

———

Saturday evening, when Jessica pulled up to the address Donna had given her, she thought her GPS must have made an error. *What the what?* Although there were plenty of cars in the parking lot, the building appeared to be deserted. She called Donna's cell. "I must've written it down wrong or something," she said. "I'm here, but this can't be it."

There was a giggle at the other end. "Hang on, I'll see if you're outside." In few seconds, Donna stepped out the front door and waved to Jessica. "Come on in!"

Jessica couldn't get over the change from exterior to interior. While the building looked all but abandoned from the parking lot, as soon as she walked in the door, she knew this was a thriving business. Behind a counter, was a little desk area, a couch, a few chairs. All the furnishings were sleek, modern and black. The lighting was dimmer than usual, the walls painted a dark red. She recognized the lobby from Donna's article. "Wow," she said. "This is the club you wrote about. What exactly is it that you do here? Or shouldn't I ask?"

Donna grabbed her purse from behind the counter. "Mostly, I just man the front door and check people in and out. It's a club—people pay by the month or year, come as often as they want to, stay as long as they want, within reason, of course. Fees go toward upkeep, new equipment. Cleanliness is a top priority, that, and privacy." She lowered her voice. "Insurance, of course. Definitely not advertising, though."

Jessica said nothing. A secret club that a lot of people, apparently, knew about. She'd had no idea that business was so good for the club, however. "So... couples only?"

Donna shrugged. "I *think* most of the members are couples, but there are single folks, too. Madame X—the owner, that's what they call her, anyway—has a website and a chat room, so members hook up there with someone they find who has... mutual interests. An elite few hook up with *her*."

"Whatever floats your boat, I suppose," Jessica said breezily. "Are any of the rooms open, so I can see one?"

They walked down the hallway. "It's early still, so there are some vacant. There are six rooms... that I know of. There may be more, but those would be private for Madame X." She lowered her voice. "She may even live here, for all I know. I never asked, but there's a locked door that may lead to an apartment. I've seen her come from that direction first thing in the morning. Here we are—"

Jessica drew in a breath. She'd always considered herself sexually adventurous, but this room obviously took it to a whole different level. "Is that for..." Her voice trailed off. A black metal contraption, a sort of swing set with chains and straps, occupied the middle of the room. She tried to imagine how one would get into the seat and what kind of positions would be possible.

"Indeed. There's another one hanging from the ceiling," Donna said, pointing overhead. She watched Jessica's face with amusement as she explained the various gizmos around the room. "The rooms are soundproof, so you'd never know from *outside* what's going on *inside*. There are panic buttons, of course, in case of emergencies, but I've never heard of them being used."

"Sometimes if I'm here just a few hours, I don't even see anyone at all," she continued, walking around the room. "They've checked in before I arrive and don't leave before my shift ends. Otherwise, I go in and get the room ready for the next folks. It all gets cleaned, equipment put back. Some people bring their own things, though. The more, um, *intimate* items."

Jessica put her hands up to the sides of her head and popped her fingers open. "Mind. Blown. I mean, I read your article, but all of this... it just didn't register." She pointed to a slender padded bench with an open headrest, more chains and restraints. The bench was slanted and looked immanently adjustable. She envisioned herself on it, face down, hands and ankles bound, Worth standing behind her, taking her. She cleared her throat and looked at her watch. "We'll be late for the movie if we don't leave now."

Did the AC go off? Without realizing it, she had started fanning herself.

Donna giggled. "Ready when you are. Let me text M and tell her I'm leaving." When they were outside, Donna locked one of the locks on the door; there were others she ignored. "Members have keys to this one," she explained. "During hours, they can let themselves in—but not to the rooms themselves. Only M and people like me have keys to keep everyone else out when the club's closed."

Jessica shook her head as they walked to her car. "It sounds like the system works smoothly," she said as they got in. "But good lord, that trapeze thing."

Unnoticed in a car, a man watched the women as they came out of the building. Whistling softly, he held up an expensive camera and snapped a series of photos. "Are those two a couple? Stranger things have happened," he mused out loud. There could be another explanation, of course, but the photo might come in handy. If nothing else, he would add it to his growing collection.

He looked around the parking lot. He was alone, now that the women had driven off. No one could see inside his van. He scanned through the digital images on his camera until he found a good one of the blonde. His timing had been perfect. Unaware he was watching, she had bent over in a skirt. The fabric was tight over her buttocks, with shapely legs coming down. *Oh, to have my hands between those. And this…*

Lance Glover unzipped his pants and let his fantasy take flight.

10

Christmas Approaches

Chet Henderson watched his bride hang ornaments on the little tabletop tree. She had convinced him that it would be better to have a small tree so there was more room for *people* on Christmas. They'd invited their nearest neighbors to meet the family in the afternoon, and they had no idea how many might show up.

Chet studied Carol as she studied the tree, carefully choosing the best spot for each trinket. Their first Christmas together, blending ornaments from their two separate lives before—it was important. Carol had spent weeks at Layla's, but for now, she was all his. Light through the window reflected off the gray in her chestnut hair, giving her an aura. "Time for a break, love."

Carol looked at the boxes of ornaments. "But there's still a lot—" Catching his eye, she understood instantly and smiled. "Oh. *That* kind of break." She hung the ornament in her hand and then sat down on his lap, snuggling against his broad chest. She unbuttoned several of the buttons on his shirt and played with the generous gray hair she found as she lifted her face for his kiss.

"I sure did miss you," he said softly.

"I can tell. You've been quite *amorous* since my return." She thought of their weekend at Keith and Layla's. "And here, we don't have to endure a twin bed!"

Chet laughed. "Yes, that was unacceptable." Attempts had been made with humorous results, but finally they had spread a blanket on the carpet and made love on the floor between the two twin beds in the guest room. When his son had knocked on the door the next morning, he'd come right in and laughed at the sight.

"Where there's a will there's a way, you always told me," Keith said. "I'm glad the accommodations were not too restrictive for you newlyweds."

Still entwined beneath the bedspread Carol had yanked off one of the beds, the couple only smiled at him. "Nothing to be embarrassed about," Chet had said later. "Keith's the one who barged in."

But now, a comfortable king-size bed awaited. Jessica had been a little concerned that the reason for the king was so they could each have their own space—she desperately wanted her mother to be happy. When she'd said as much, Carol had put her fears to rest. "Don't worry, sweetie. We sleep in the middle. And use the rest of the space for *other* activities."

Arm in arm, the two walked into the bedroom. "Undress for me?" Chet asked.

It never ceased to amaze Carol. She and Greg had had a wonderful marriage; his death two years before had been devastating. It had taken her a year before she even considered involvement with another man to be the remotest possibility, but once Chet had asked her to dinner the first time, that was "all she wrote" as Greg would've said. Even then, she had lacked the imagination to envision another relationship as passionate as the one she'd enjoyed with Greg—perhaps even more passionate. She shook her head at the thought, and Chet mistook it for a denial.

"No?" Ironically, his thoughts had run along the same lines as Carol's, watching her trim the tree. His and Angie's marriage had not had the spark Carol and Greg's had had, but they were friendly and mostly compatible. Their union had produced two terrific children, but Angie had never enjoyed the physical aspect as much as he had. It had overshadowed his own pleasure to a significant degree. He had wanted so badly to please his wife, but what pleased her most was infrequency, not a new position.

He had adapted, appreciating their history together, mourning her death. But this. This woman. She came from a different mold. And they were both in their sixties! *Does this ever happen?* When he'd said that to Carol, she had simply said, "I think it's *supposed* to be this way. It just rarely is."

Carol smiled and winked at him now. "Not *no, silly.* Yes. Of course, yes." As she spoke, she slowly unbuttoned her blouse. She pulled off the sweatpants she'd kept on after their morning walk in the brisk December air. Her shoes had been left just inside the door, but she pulled her socks off now. He blinked lazily as he watched her, intent on every move.

For a few seconds, Carol stood motionless, making room for his anticipation. When he opened his mouth just a fraction, she'd know to proceed. Some things shouldn't be rushed. *There.* Carol reached behind her back with both hands and unhooked her bra—not a lacy, sexy bra for walking and tree decorating, but a sensible white thing that had seen better days. Chet did not seem to mind at all as her ample breasts broke free.

A little shyly, Carol looked downward as she wriggled out of equally sensible white cotton panties. She'd never been one for what she considered "big girl" panties, but these were merely functional, nothing fancy. She knew, though, that despite the extras—a few extra pounds, some stretchmarks and wrinkles around her eyes, a bit of cellulite—in Chet's opinion, she was everything he wanted in a woman. She smiled directly at him, confident and secure, almost daring him to just sit there when she stood naked, just out of reach.

"Do you know what I love the most about your body?" he asked softly.

Carol bit her lip, her eyes sparkling. She cupped her breasts with her hands, pressing them into a younger, perkier version. "These?"

He shook his head slowly.

She giggled and dropped her hands to her waist, spinning around before bending over slightly with her hands on her buttocks. "These?"

"Uh-uh."

Carol rolled her eyes, enjoying the moment every bit as much as her husband. What woman *wouldn't* enjoy feeling adored and cherished? She made a show of thinking deeply before slowly running her hands down to the salt-and-pepper triangle that, as surely as an X on a treasure map, marked the spot. "This? Is this what you love the most?" she whispered.

He surprised her by once again shaking his head in the negative before moving to her, embracing her. "What I love the most about your body is everything… and the fact that it's yours. And the fact that it's mine."

Retired though he was, Chet still worked out at the fire department gym. Scooping her up in his arms, he laid her gently on the bed. When he lay down beside her, he let out a sigh of contentment. "Maybe we should just take a little nap instead," he murmured.

Carol snorted as she laid a hand on his jeans. "Absolutely not. Not with *that* big thing wanting to get out." Giggling, she undid his zipper so he could shimmy out of his jeans and boxers. When he was nude, she reached across him for a bottle of lubricant on the nightstand.

When they'd first been intimate, Chet had—he admitted later—felt he'd let her down because she needed "lube", but she had convinced him it was an age thing, *not* a desire thing. She squirted a few drops into her hand and warmed it with the other before lovingly applying it to his erection. Once he knew this only enhanced her eventual pleasure, they included it in their foreplay.

Sometimes, he insisted on lubricating her instead, either by caressing her "lady parts" as he called them, or by using his mouth and tongue to get her wet. Other times, her body decided it was still a teenager after all, and as they played around, his cock slipped in easily, surprising them both. "Well!" he'd say with a touch of pride. "That was easy!"

Today, he caressed her back and teased her breasts as she massaged the slippery warming fluid over the head of his penis and down the sides. Carol gripped him harder and then whispered, "Turn over, Chief."

He faced her as she rested her leg on his hip and guided his cock into her body. The moment of union—the joining, the oneness—was always such bliss for her. They lay still for a few seconds, just enjoying their closeness. Then Chet kissed her long and completely, their tongues playing, becoming joined by mouths just as they were below. Without losing either connection, they rolled over so that Chet was on top as he began to move, slowly at first, then more quickly. "Mmm. Oh yes, *yes*," Carol groaned softly.

He slowed again, concentrating on Carol. In answer, she grabbed his buttocks tightly, pulling him in more deeply.

Chet bent down, kissing her neck, her chest, nipping at her nipples as Carol gripped even harder. Her legs wrapped around him as her hands grabbed his head, forcing him to kiss her on the mouth as she arched her back and let out a moan of ecstasy. Only then did Chet thrust hard and fast, reaching his own climax within seconds. His face grimaced in concentration as he uttered a deep moan of release, relaxed with a sigh and then raised himself off, elbows straight, so he could look at her. "You are so beautiful," he said.

"You're just saying that because I put out," she teased, obviously pleased.

"That's right," he said as he bent down to kiss her. "I tell that to all the soon-to-be grandmothers who spread their legs for me."

That gave Carol the giggles, silent giggles making her whole body shake. Chet wiggled his eyebrows lasciviously. "Oh I like that. Keep shaking and I may just feel the earth move again."

Instead, Carol pinched both of his butt cheeks.

"Ow!" he cried. "Okay, you little vixen, now you've done it." With one smooth movement, Chet was off her, pulling her onto his stomach where he trapped her feet. "You've been a naughty girl." He spanked her lightly with one hand a few times and then pulled her higher by both arms so that her breasts were above his face. Chuckling, he took first one nipple in his mouth, biting it gently, and then the other before laying Carol back on the bed. His gaze moved swiftly up and down her curves. "If we don't stop now, you're going to have to endure me again."

Carol laughed. "It was your idea!" Chet got up and dressed quickly as she did the same. They embraced, still feeling the heat of their lovemaking. A lingering, wet kiss and Carol pushed him away. "If we don't stop now, you're going to have to endure *me* again."

Her phone rang from where she'd left it in the living room, and she ran to answer it. "Keith? What's wrong?"

Several miles away, Worth and Jessica wrapped presents and enjoyed homemade eggnog. "I love this time of year," Jessica said as she filled out a tag for Worth's mother Molly. She smiled across the table to him. "And I love signing things 'Worth and Jessica'. It's still hard for me to believe."

"I *know*! This time last year, we settled for phone calls and not much else. Now we're Mr. and Mrs. Worth Vincent. I never get tired of saying it," Worth replied. He held up a gift card to Baby Gap. "Now whoever could *this* be for?"

Jessica chuckled as she wrapped the delicate wool scarf for her mother she'd bought while shopping for her wedding dress in Paris. Molly had set the whole trip up—a wedding gift from her and her current love interest Fred. "Layla's feeling very well, and the doctor says she and baby are both *doing* well, but she's getting antsy. Cabin fever. Almost a month of bed rest, poor thing, and another to go."

Worth got up to refill their glasses. "Her sister's coming soon, isn't she?"

"Already here, which is good news for Mom and Chet." She gave Worth a knowing look. "*Great* news for Mom and Chet."

Worth grinned as he handed her more eggnog and sat again. "Those two." He reached for one of her hands to squeeze. "I hope that when we're their age, we still enjoy each other as much as they seem to. Do you think that's possible?"

Jessica returned the squeeze. "We found each other under almost impossible circumstances, solved multiple murders, cleared your name and got married, all within one year's time. I think *anything's* possible." She thought again of Layla and breathed a quick prayer for her safety and that of her baby. *I hope a baby for Worth is possible. He never thought he'd find love, much less have a family.*

Her phone rang on the table. "Hey, Mom. We were just talking about you," Jessica answered brightly.

"Layla's gone into labor. We're on our way to the hospital now."

11

Christmas in Florida

"You've got to be kidding me, Roy," Eric said as he met the driver in front of the Steins' mansion. Instead of the Lincoln Town Car that had picked him up at the airport in November, apparently they were taking a stretch limo to fetch Donna.

Although the Asian man's name was actually Hiroya, he'd instructed Eric to use his nickname. A slender man, with short black hair, he wore his chauffeur's "uniform"—a neat black suit with white shirt and black tie and a black cap. "Mr. Stein insisted. Said you have been gone from your new wife too long for the Town Car."

"What's that got to do with anything?" Eric was confused. "I'll ride up front on the way there."

"You'll see."

The two chatted easily as they made the drive to Orlando International Airport. Roy told him that depending on the trip, the Steins sometimes took charter flights from the closer and smaller Vero airport and sometimes used the medium-sized airport in Melbourne, just to the north. The drive was fairly boring as far as view, but interesting as far as conversation.

Roy was born in the U.S. to a Japanese mother and Caucasian father, 'inheriting his good looks from his mother,' he said with a chuckle. His name meant "great esteem."

"I like that," said Eric, watching cows feed along the highway. He hadn't realized that Florida was cattle country. "And Asahi means 'morning sunshine'." Instinctively, he glanced at Roy to gauge his reaction.

At the sound of his co-worker's name, Roy closed his eyes for a split-second and smiled. "Ah, yes. Asahi. The beautiful Asahi."

Eric was intrigued. Asahi was not what he would call beautiful, but there was no accounting for taste. Jessica was womanly and curvy, but it was the small-breasted, almost boyish Donna who had stolen his heart, who could make that heart race. Perhaps he had made too quick a judgment on the sweet cook's appearance. He certainly didn't agree with her own assessment of being too *pochapocha* for the naturist party. *I'm glad she wasn't there, though. It's hard enough looking the Steins in the eye now that I've seen them naked.*

During the trip from the airport a few weeks before, Eric had also ridden in the front seat, but he and Roy had talked mostly about Florida, the weather, and various sports teams. Eric was learning to appreciate the fine art of small talk to a greater degree since meeting Donna, but Roy had been the one to keep things going then. Now Eric dug deeper.

"So. Asahi. Have you two ever dated? I mean you practically live together; at least you're at the same house."

Roy shook his head. "I was dating someone else when I began working for the Steins last summer and had little interaction with her. I tend to be busy outside, and she stays inside. Not much communication. When we do talk, she's a bit standoffish. Very cool."

When Eric told him about the naturist party, the *pochapocha*, and the cougars, Roy laughed heartily. "I had the night off by design, too. No way do I want to run into the Steins *au naturale*, although I've been called to their suite plenty of times when they were. They explained it all up front; it just doesn't happen that often. Not that it would have been a deal breaker." He took one hand off the steering wheel to rub his thumb against his other fingers. "They pay very well, as you know."

The men were silent for several miles before Roy spoke again. "She thinks she's too big? Really? I think Asahi is the perfect shape and size." Roy cleared his throat. "Now that I'm single again, perhaps I should test the water."

Meeting Donna had changed Eric's life—and learning of her particular inclinations and abilities had turned his world upside down. "You should. You'll never know how deep the water is until you dive in."

For the rest of the two-hour drive, the men were quieter. Soon the airport's *Arrivals* sign was overhead. A text had alerted Eric—Donna was through baggage claim and waiting on the sidewalk. "There she is!" he said excitedly. He rolled the window down and called to her as Roy slowed the limo, easing over to the curb.

Eric jumped out as soon as he could do so safely, embracing Donna enthusiastically. Roy discreetly took her bag and opened the door to the back section of the car. As Eric led Donna by the hand, he ducked down to look inside, standing up quickly. "Wow!"

Roy smiled as they stepped inside. "I told you."

Donna and Eric looked around the limo in amazement. There was a TV, mini-bar, enough room for a dozen people. A curtained window divided the driver's area from that of the passengers. Soft jazz played in the background.

Eric shook his head. "You weren't kidding. This is great. Oh, Donna, meet Roy, Hiroya. He's taking off after he drops us at the house. Where're you headed? I forgot."

"My folks live in Miami, so I've got another two-hour drive

ahead of me—not that you two lovebirds need a third wheel around." He closed the door and drove off with a smile.

Donna and Eric sat holding hands, still taking in the surroundings. Finally, Donna whispered, "Are you sure he can't hear us? Or see us?"

Eric poured two flutes of champagne that Roy had put on ice for them at Mrs. Stein's direction. "I'm sure."

When they clinked their crystal together, Donna said, "To privacy and lots of room!"

Eric chuckled. "To *two* hours alone with my wife after much *too* long!"

Within minutes, clothing was scattered all around the car and they had spread a throw thoughtfully provided on the seat. Donna murmured appreciatively at Eric's tanned physique but then scowled. "What a minute… where are your tan lines?"

Eric was a little sheepish. "After the Thanksgiving party, I thought I should take care of my Casper-colored butt. The Steins' private beach is usually vacant. And definitely vacant now. Of course, we might be able to arrange a ride to the nude beach south of it."

In answer, Donna shifted on the seat so that she sat on her knees straddling his lap. "Yours is the only naked body I want to see—the only body of *any* kind I want to see—for as long as I can." Worth had given her a full two weeks off with pay, but she planned to fly back home with Eric whenever the fireplace was finished, vacation time or not.

Eric stroked her back as she adjusted him so that she could snuggle up against his erection, feeling his heat emanating. He'd had a semi since they arrived at the airport, but now he was standing tall. Donna reached down to stroke him softly, then harder, leaning in for a kiss. "Oh how I've missed you." She fingered the head of his penis gently, smoothing a pearl of fluid all around.

Without a word, Donna eased onto the floor, still on her

knees, and took him in her mouth. Up and down, up and down, sucking vigorously, she occasionally stopped to bite him gently, or to trace the circumference of his head with her tongue, all the while murmuring, "Do you like this? How about this?"

Donna and Eric had enjoyed oral stimulation as part of their sex play, but although Donna had climaxed, he had never come. Whether due to an old taboo or personal preference, they had never discussed it. Now, however, Eric was lost in the incredible waves of pleasure Donna was giving him. He wanted to pull her up so that he could suck on her nipples. But. This. Felt. So. Good.

Donna stopped to lick his inner thighs and scrotum, whispering, "Do you want to finish this way?" as she resumed sucking, now reaching with one hand to stimulate herself. When he only moaned a little in response, she sucked more intensely, her hands moved more intensely, until her mouth filled with warm fluid. She could feel him tremble against her cheeks. When she swallowed, the taste was slightly fruity, slightly metallic.

"Good lord," Eric muttered, his head resting on the seat back.

Donna straddled him again, pulling his hands up to her breasts as she continued to rock gently in his lap. "You liked that, didn't you?" *He's still hard enough*, she thought. Dropping her feet to the floor of the car for leverage, she stuffed his softening penis inside of her, violently rocking now as he gripped her buttocks, keeping the connection, desperate for her own release. When it came, she all but howled with ecstasy. "Yesss, yes, yes, oh god, *yes!*"

Still hovering over his face, she kissed Eric long and hard. "I love you, sweet man."

"I love you back. That was... wonderful. You are. Wonderful."

Giggling, Donna sat beside him and draped her legs across his lap, leaning her head against his arm. "We are wonderful together."

Eric looked out the window. "Uh oh. We'd better get dressed. I think we're approaching the turn-off." He grinned at Donna. "But you? A turn *on* all the way." He chuckled. "I suppose I'll have to wear clothes to work on the fireplace, even though no one else will be at the house, for safety's sake if nothing else. But feel free to try the naturist lifestyle yourself for the next few weeks while you watch. I won't mind a bit."

When they reached the Steins' house, Roy put Donna's bag just inside the atrium while Eric gave her a little tour. Roy went to his room for his backpack then found the couple to say his goodbyes. He told them he'd be riding his motorcycle to Miami and had clothes that stayed at his parents' house. "Merry Christmas," he called over his shoulder as he walked to the garage for his bike.

"You too!" They watched as he roared off, stopping to lock the gate behind himself before taking a left on the highway.

"We're alone—in a multi-million-dollar mansion," Eric said, shaking his head.

"What *will* we do to pass the time?"

The next ten days passed quickly, however, as if in a dream. There was no need to go anywhere other than the bedroom, bathroom, and kitchen, but Donna challenged Eric to make love to her in every room of the house—the ones they could enter, anyway. The servants' hallway was locked, as was the Steins' private wing. They were careful to respect the furniture and keep everything tidy, but their sense of adventure and variety was satisfied fully. The clock meant nothing. Mealtimes meant nothing. When they wanted to eat, they ate. When they wanted to sleep, they slept. Between sex and work at all hours of the day and night, they explored the estate and talked and swam and sunned.

Christmas came and went. Sitting on the beach, they told each other stories of childhood Christmases—Eric's full of presents and family feasts, Donna's full of disappointment and loneliness. Tears were shed and kissed gently away as the moon rose over the ocean. For them, the real gift was being together again.

Donna kept in touch with Jessica and knew that Layla had given birth to a tiny, but healthy baby girl. After a few tense hours, all was well. Layla's sister would remain until she had to return to her school after the first. The baby of Layla and Keith had taken priority over the babe in the manger this year, but the families had all managed to be together on Christmas Day. Chet and Carol's neighborhood gathering had also been a success.

Now, Donna sat on the loveseat they had carried into the great room so that she could keep Eric company a little closer as he worked near the ceiling. Some eighteen feet high, the wall was a testament both to nature and also his skill. Italian stone of many tones of brown and amber were arranged in a free-form pattern. Because the fireplace was electric, there was no need for a chimney, but the wall added elegance and drama to Doris Stein's addition. The mantle, also of stone, would soon provide a home for priceless figurines, plants, photos or candles.

"That doesn't look safe to me," she called up to Eric. "Are you sure you tightened everything?"

"No worries, m'lady. The last stone! I can hardly believe it. I finished in record time, despite your *numerous* interruptions," he called back.

Eric tapped the final stone into place. The end of a job was always satisfying. But of course, the job was not over quite yet. Even though he had tooled the joints and washed mortar off the stones as he went, there was now the task of sealing the entire wall. He had plenty of time before the Steins returned. He stopped to lean on the crossbar, calling down to her, "I think we should cele—"

Donna screamed as the crossbar gave way, sending Eric over the side. He landed on a pile of empty mortar bags which did little to break his fall. Running to him, Donna thought at first that he was gone. "Eric, nooo," she cried, checking for a pulse. Concrete dust from the bags had billowed up and settled onto both of them.

Groaning, Eric stirred. "Well, that was unfortunate," he muttered. "Thank God I put padding down to protect the floor, anyway." He tried to move his extremities, one at a time. Left leg, right leg, right arm… "Ow! I think I sprained it."

Donna moved the bags away, her face suddenly pale. "You broke it, Eric. What can I do?"

Carefully, she helped him rise and get to the loveseat. He was dusty and dirty, and the fabric would suffer for it, but who cared? "Smart house," he mumbled before passing out from the pain.

Smart house. Smart house. She'd written an article about smart houses, but she hadn't set her voice up here. How sensitive was this one? "Call Ari Stein," she said loudly.

"Dialing Ari Stein," a lilting voice answered. The next voice she heard was Mr. Stein's.

"Mr. Stein! Thank God. This is Eric's wife Donna. We've got a problem."

Ari would disengage the gate lock remotely, he said, and call an ambulance right away with directions. It would take at least thirty minutes for it to arrive, though. "Hang in there, Donna! Help is on the way. Doris says keep him warm and stay calm. I'm so sorry, but there's no way for us to get back sooner than planned. Will you be okay? Should I contact someone to come help you?"

"Thank you, but not yet. I'll see what the hospital says," Donna said, feeling strange to be talking to the ceiling. "I *think* it's a broken arm, but there could be internal damage. He might have to stay." It was too soon to tell.

When the call was over, she googled first aid on her phone and gently laid Eric on his back, running to the living room for pillows to support his head and knees. The loveseat was too short to accommodate his entire body, but it was the best she could do. She dampened a towel in the kitchen and filled a glass with water. Gently wiping his face and dripping some water onto his lips, she prayed, making deals as people do. "If you'll just help him, I'll..." then stopped. "I'll what?" she said out loud. "Love him more? How could I?" A dozen childhood lessons and sermons flooded her mind. *If it be Thy will. Why wouldn't it be? Please, Father.*

Father. At the very word, bile rose in her throat. Donna's mother had left her alone with her father when she was six. She didn't even know the day her mother had died from an overdose. But she knew exactly the date and time her father began molesting her. It was her twelfth birthday.

12

Healings of Different Kinds

E ric sat on the loveseat giving orders. A cold drink and snacks were within reach. His feet were propped up, and a favorite band provided background music. His left arm was in a cast and the painkillers were effective without muddying his mind. *And,* he thought, *I have the loveliest of views.*

After their return to the estate from the emergency room in Sebastian—home of the closest hospital—Eric had dozed; Donna had cleaned. Whenever he was awake, she pampered him with food and kisses and—eventually—somewhat awkward lovemaking. When he napped, she worked. It had taken hours, but the bags were gone, the dust swept up. She'd managed, with great difficulty, to move the scaffolding to one side, so that now, the wall could be fully appreciated. The wall was not what Eric admired at the moment, however.

The final task was sealing the stone wall. A sprayer might be used, but Eric had not rented one yet. Rather than wait, he opted to use a roller. Donna found one with a handy extension in the little building that housed equipment and tools, but when Eric tried to manage it with one hand, he was quickly discouraged.

"I can do it," Donna suggested. She was on a ladder now, working quickly and efficiently. She was perhaps five feet off the ground, wearing only a large t-shirt of Eric's, so she didn't ruin any of her clothes. She hadn't exactly packed for manual labor. She backed down from the ladder to get a rag and saw him looking. Slowly and purposefully, she bent over, glancing around to grin at him.

"I'm sure I look *very* sexy in this getup," she said with a giggle. Her hair was a mess, she was sweaty, and the sealer had sprinkled all over her.

In answer, Eric stood up and walked slowly toward her.

"Oh no, mister. I've got work to do." Donna's back was to the ladder and she started stepping up. He caught up to her when she was a few feet above him.

"Is that right?" he said, following her up the ladder. Balancing himself, he took his good hand and reached under the shirt, finding her lace panties. He ducked his head beneath the edge of the shirt and grabbed the top of the panties with his teeth. As he backed down the ladder, the panties pulled off.

Taking them from his mouth and throwing them at her playfully, he said, "I'll leave you alone to your work now." For the next hour, he sat and watched, relishing the hint of bottom that emerged from time to time. Finally, he could stand it no longer. "Break time," he called. "You're torturing me."

Donna laughed. "I think I've done all I can do for now anyway. Tomorrow, we should try two ladders. One of us can man the sealer, the other a brush. I'm past where the roller will work, am I not?"

She turned around slightly and seductively pulled the shirt to her waist. "But what I need is a shower. I am *so dirty*." She winked, teasing him.

"A dirty girl sounds fine to me, but so does a shower," Eric said as he stood. "You soap me up, and I promise to hang my arm outside the door, so it doesn't get wet."

"Soap you up?" Donna cooed as she stepped off the ladder and walked into his arms. "I'll do a lot more than that."

The Steins were thrilled with the stone wall. The household was back to normal only a few days before New Year's Eve. It was arranged that Donna and Eric would fly home January second so that they could attend the party to christen the new addition. And no, the Steins had assured them, this was not a party for the naturist society, but business associates and family.

Workers and decorators were everywhere, preparing, painting, cleaning. "It's amazing what gets done when a person says, 'Money's no object'," Donna observed dryly as she perched on a stool in the kitchen.

Asahi laughed. "You are correct, Donna-san. Where is your husband?"

Donna was annoyed. After being apart, she'd expected to spend every possible moment with Eric, but today, he had gone on an errand with Roy instead. Roy! He could have at least asked her to join them.

Instead of grousing, however, she stretched her back and took a sip of tea. Asahi, at her request, was teaching her new tastes, new Japanese dishes and customs. *Such a sweet person.* Eric had told her of Roy's own opinion. "Roy is very good-looking, don't you think?"

Is she blushing? Donna smiled. "I mean, he's not really *my* type, but…"

As expected, Asahi frowned as she worked. "Hiroya is quite handsome. And he is courteous and brave also. And smart. Why he would not be a woman's type, I would not know."

Donna nodded. "I just meant he isn't Eric, that's all."

Asahi considered this. "Oh. Well." She began her work again, carefully slicing tuna for sashimi.

As Donna finished her tea, Eric and Roy came into the kitchen, each carrying something out of view. When Roy sidled up to Asahi and cleared his throat, she held her knife up to him in mock threat. "Yes, Hiroya? What can I do for you?"

Roy pulled a beautiful bouquet of flowers from behind his back. "You can accompany me to the Steins' party. I have already spoken with them and they are hiring extra servers so that you have nothing to do that night but stay by my side."

Asahi's eyes sparkled. So quietly that Donna could barely hear her speak, she said, "I will go with you to the party, Hiroya." She took the flowers and bowed. "Thank you for the flowers. They are beautiful."

Roy gave her a little bow in return. "As is the one who holds them." He winked at Eric and excused himself as Asahi searched for a vase.

Donna was glad Eric had gone with Roy—he probably needed that encouragement to make a move. *That was worth missing him for a few hours.*

"And for you, babe," Eric said, handing her a white box.

Donna put the box on the island and opened it. Inside, was a beautiful fuchsia sundress and matching scarf, large enough that it could serve as a wrap on a chilly night. "It's gorgeous! But how did—"

"You think I don't know my wife's size by now?" Eric scoffed. "Plus, I checked all your labels and guessed. I knew you were expecting us to be home by now. You wouldn't have packed a party dress. Or these..." He lifted up the dress to reveal a pair of delicate sandals the exact color of the dress, as well as intricate silver earrings and matching choker. It all looked very expensive.

He saw the question in her eyes. "I haven't told you what I got paid," he whispered in her ear.

The flight back home was Donna's first experience flying first class. "I could get used to this," she murmured as she settled into the roomy seat.

"A few more jobs like that one and you can," Eric said.

Donna's eyes flashed as she sat up. "Oh, no, you don't. I am not going to sit at home missing you while you go gallivanting all over the world laying Italian-fucking-stone."

Eric hushed her with a kiss. "You won't have to. One of the businessmen at the party has an office in the city and wants to build a home there too. Lots of stonework. Lots of connections. He thinks he can keep me very busy." He paused. "We might even be able to start looking for a house of our own. We *might* even think about starting a family one of these days."

Donna beamed, resting back in the seat for takeoff. *A house. A home. A real home. Children.* Was she ready for that? What kind of father would Eric be? *Father.* She was surprised to feel a tear roll down her cheek. "Oh, Eric." She began to cry quietly.

Immediately, he was concerned. "What's the matter?"

For the remainder of the flight, Donna painfully but thoroughly took Eric through her childhood memories. Her mother's addiction, her dad's drinking. On her twelfth birthday, he had taken her out for ice cream. As they walked along the sidewalk outside, licking their cones, he had said, "You're really growing up, you know."

"That meant so much to me," Donna said. Her tiny breasts probably didn't need a bra yet, but she had begged just the same. She had started her period. She'd even had a growth spurt. Still shorter than most of the girls in her class, there was real hope of catching up eventually. And she was so proud of her father, this tall, burly man who had raised her. He drank too much, but what was too much, really? He only spanked her if she was really naughty, and never too hard. He gave her an allowance for doing all the cleaning and the cooking.

"I was okay, even without a mother, until that night," Donna sniffled. "*We* were okay." She paused to blow her nose.

Eric hoped silently that he didn't know what was coming next; he had a sinking feeling that he did. "Until?"

Donna's head fell back, and she closed her eyes, seeing it all too clearly. "After we got home, I undressed and put on my nightgown, brushed my teeth, brushed my hair a hundred times, all the things twelve-year-old girls do. I called goodnight to him and climbed into bed." She bit her lip. "After a few minutes, he came to my room. He climbed into bed with me. I could smell the liquor on his breath when he kissed me on the cheek. He kept saying he loved me. He loved me so much. I-I didn't know he was doing anything wrong. Not yet."

Eric stopped her with his hand. "You don't have to tell me anything else. I think I have a pretty good picture."

She shook her head and frowned. "I've never told *anyone*, Eric. I have to finally tell someone, and it has to be you. Don't you see? I'm still letting him hurt me by keeping it all inside. Maybe that's what appealed to me at the club... I have this rage inside that I've hung onto."

Eric frowned. Would sharing her story with him impact their relationship? He enjoyed things the way they were. But she clearly was in pain. "Go on, then."

"It hurt. How could it not? He was a grown man. But he was also gentle. He told me it would get easier the more we did it. I didn't even know what 'it' was. No mother, no instructions. I was so stupid, so naive..."

"You were a child," Eric said roughly. His hands had clenched as she spoke quietly and calmly of the abuse. "Is he still alive? Because right now I'd like to—"

Donna laid a hand on the fist not partially encased in the cast. "He died when I was eighteen," she said in a soothing tone. "I'd left home at sixteen, moved in with a friend from school, told her family it was because of the drinking. And he never asked me to come home." Her voice was low. "Sometimes I wonder if he'd still be alive if I hadn't left. Maybe I should have just endured it for his sake. Or told someone... but he'd have gone to prison, and I didn't want that. God help me, he was a monster, but he was a kind one. You have to understand that, Eric. He was never cruel to me."

Eric shook his head and repeated himself, "You. Were. A. Child."

Donna nodded and smiled sadly. "I'm not a child any more, Eric. And I can't live with rage. I've hidden it. I've even used it. But just saying the words out loud? I see that he was in pain. I was the closest thing to my mom that he could reach. I even looked like her. The alcohol was a factor. His loneliness. My loneliness." She saw the disapproval in his face. "I'm *not* excusing what he did, Eric. But maybe I've started to finally forgive him. For all I know, he was abused himself. My mom, too, maybe. They didn't know how to deal with their pain. I don't want to carry mine any longer."

Eric was silent as an announcement came over the sound system. They'd be landing soon. His arm throbbed. *Two more weeks of this damn cast.* Selfishly, he wondered if Donna's new attitude would affect him negatively. Had he been a surrogate, the father figure she loved to whip? *Things have been so good between us and now this.* He sighed deeply, but the sound of the airplane's engine masked it.

"You look great!" Jessica gushed, twirling Donna around the next day at the office. "What's different? Tanner, for sure. Your biceps look more toned, too."

Donna laughed. "Well, we did get out in the sun a bit— Florida is *great*, and you wouldn't *believe* the house we stayed in." She curled one arm beside her head. "Welcome to the gun show," she said with a giggle. "These muscles are well-earned, let me tell you."

Jessica shook her head. "I am so thankful Eric wasn't hurt worse, Donna. When I think what might have happened…"

Donna hugged her friend. "I know. With Layla, too." Just arrived at the office, they were getting coffee in the break area. "How is the baby doing?"

In answer, Jessica pulled out her phone and showed Donna her latest photos. "So sweet. Angela Michelle, after Keith's mother. She was in the NICU for a few days but did so well, they're both home now. The doctor thinks maybe Layla was even further along than they'd thought. At any rate, everything's copacetic."

"Copa-what?" Lance Glover had stepped into the room unnoticed. "Welcome home, Donna*let*." He pulled two camera lenses out of his fishing vest and held them up to his eyes like mismatched binoculars. "Look, ladies—I'm a Peeping Tom!" A few coworkers in the room laughed at the joke.

Donna did not. Her eyebrows shot up, but she said nothing. Obviously ignoring him, she nodded to Jessica as she walked out. "Back to work!"

Jessica followed, whispering loudly as they walked, "What's that all about?"

Donna shrugged. "I don't like him, and I think I just figured out why."

"Well?"

"He reminds me of my father."

"Did everything go all right at the doctor, babe?" Donna asked when Eric called that afternoon.

"Right as rain," he replied. "Two more weeks, just like the doc in Florida said. I can do anything I feel like, but I think I'll

wait on calling the guy about the stone until the cast is off."
They discussed dinner plans, which reminded Donna to let
Madame X know she was back, in case she was needed to fill
in for a few hours. She'd made it clear that she couldn't work
much, not on top of the magazine, and that it was just until
Eric was back, anyway, but if she was needed here and there,
she didn't mind.

"Which babe was at the doctor?" Lance was watching her
lazily from the cubicle at her back, eavesdropping on the call.
"The man-babe or the lady-babe?"

"The what?" Donna whipped around in her chair.

Lance crossed his arms and was smug. "I saw you and boss
lady come out of that club a few weeks ago, that's all. Looked
like something more than friends."

Donna smiled in spite of herself. *I'm not angry,* she thought
with surprise. *He's just a dickhead who thinks he has everything figured
out. The rage is gone. What do you know?* Instead of a sharp retort,
Donna laughed. "Boy, do you have it wrong. I'm as hetero as
they come, happily married, thank you very much. My
husband broke his arm over Christmas if you must know. Stop
hovering, Lance. Don't you have some photos to shoot?"

A few heads turned their way, but Lance just shrugged.
"My bad. Whatever you say, Donna*let*."

Walking back to the photo room, Lance's mind returned to the
club. Maybe she hadn't been there with Jessica, but she was
there. *And hubby's out of commission.*

13

Things Come to a Head

Several nights later, Donna worked late at the magazine. Engrossed in typing up a profile on a most interesting city councilwoman, the hours slipped away. When she finally looked up from her laptop, she was surprised to see an empty room. The custodian had left the lights on, but she vaguely remembered him sweeping around her within the last few hours. She packed her things. A night watchman for the entire building would be by later to check on things, but she would lock up anyway.

No sooner had she flipped the main switch for the room than she remembered the half a sub in the break room refrigerator she'd intended to take home for Eric. Navigating from years of experience working there, she easily made it to the break room in the darkened office. One arm was encumbered with a notebook and both purse and laptop case straps. She opened the fridge with the other and reached in for the sandwich bag.

As she bent over, Lance Glover appeared from a dark corner. Suddenly, one arm cinched around her waist, pinning her to him. Backing up, she was helpless to do anything but step back with him in an awkward, frightening dance. The refrigerator door shut, and they were in almost total darkness. Only the red lights of the exit signs in various places around the room, and the hallway lighting coming in from a fixed window beside the main door, were evident.

Donna still didn't know for sure who had her, but she could guess. "Let me go this minute," she hissed. "It's not funny."

Lance had an iron grip on her left arm and now hooked her right arm tightly, speaking quietly into her ear. "No, it's not funny at all. But you've heard several people laugh at me because of you. *You* laughed at me the other day. But you're not laughing now, are you?"

Think, Donna. The guard will come around soon. Keep him talking until then. "I'm sorry, Lance. I didn't mean to hurt you. You're new here. We joke around. You'll see. I didn't mean anything by it, honest."

"Let me tell you about honesty, Donna*let*. And then you're going to *let* me do what I've been wanting to do to you since the day we met. Remember, Donna*let*? You were in line at the copier with pretty Paul, but you were flirting with me."

"I was no—"

Lance pulled her tighter into his twisted embrace, and she could feel his erection at her back. *Where is that guard?* "Yes, I flirted with you. I'm sorry if you got the wrong idea, though. I was about to be married—"

"And then you bent over in front of me that day; you had to have known I was looking. I could practically smell your cooch from where I was. I'll bet you didn't even wear panties that day." With a quick move, he pinned both her arms with one of his so that he could reach between her legs.

Thank God I wore slacks today. That will take up some time.

"Hmm," he said. "I can't tell if you're wearing them now or not, but I'll know soon enough." His voice was thick with desire.

Good. Get as hard and needy as you can, dickhead. You'll have to kill me first.

"Everything all right in there?" There was a flash of light. The night watchman had found the door open and heard voices.

Lance released his grip, but not before warning her, "I was just kidding, of course. Don't make a big deal out of anything, or you'll be sorry."

Donna fairly ran out of the break room, greeting the guard with a big smile. "Hey! Yes, all's well. Working a little late, that's all. Listen… this late, would you be a dear and walk me out to my car? I'm a little wary of going alone."

The guard frowned as Lance came toward them. Donna could see the wheels turning in his mind and nodded toward Lance. "He would, of course, but he's going the other way and is already running late."

The guard shrugged. "Sure. No problem at all."

Only when Donna was safely locked inside her car and out onto the open street, did she breathe easily. She'd always been afraid something like this would happen, had always been careful to stay in groups, to never be caught alone in the dark… *like I was on my twelfth birthday.* She gasped. *I've been afraid of my father all this time, but he's dead.* Another very alive man had accosted her tonight. *And I wasn't afraid. I knew the guard would come.* She breathed a prayer of thanks.

Tomorrow, she would explain the whole thing to Worth, she decided as she drove. *One less photographer at the magazine by tomorrow evening.* A thought occurred to her. *Should I tell Eric?* Physically, he was not in the best shape for confrontation. It occurred to her that Eric's personality was naturally passive, too. She'd seen him disappointed and disapproving and concerned, but not really angry. The angriest she'd seen him was on the plane, when she told him about her father—and that was because of her age more than anything. He'd told her

Lance was nothing to worry about. *He wouldn't do anything, not that there's anything to do. Lance will deny it all. I can't prove anything. It's my word against his.*

Unbidden, another voice spoke deep inside. *What proof could you have shown about your father? Mightn't he have found a way to turn it all against you? You were just a child, making stories up because he wouldn't let you have your way.*

Donna took a deep breath. Of course, she would tell Eric. But after she spoke with Worth. That would surely put an end to things.

"Are you sure you have to leave, Kris? We love having you here." Layla nursed little Angela in the rocking chair of her bedroom. Her younger sister was folding laundry on the bed, carefully putting it in a basket as she did.

"We do!" Keith called from the nearby kitchen. "You've been a tremendous help."

Kristina Myers smiled shyly. "You're sweet to say so, and I've loved it—well, I loved it when I knew you and Angela were going to be okay. Up to that point, I was terrified."

Layla switched the baby to the other side and adjusted her robe. Breastfeeding was such an intimate, satisfying experience. She never would have guessed. "Did you know that the same hormone released during orgasm is released during nursing?"

Kristina blushed and giggled quietly as she worked. "No. I suppose that explains why you nurse so often."

Layla laughed softly. It was good to hear Kristina giggle—she'd gotten so *serious* this past year. When she'd arrived, Layla had actually been shocked by Kristina's appearance. Formerly vivacious and outgoing, meticulous with her makeup, hair, and clothes, Kristina was now painfully quiet. Clean, but a bit disheveled. Something had happened to change her, or was it the strain of working with challenging students? She and Keith had both tried to coax more information from her during her visit, but Kristina was well-versed in deflecting questions or avoiding conflict. Plus, they'd had other things on their minds, with the baby.

"I nurse often because this wee girl is hungry *all* the time," Layla said, stroking her daughter's pink cheek. "Every two hours around the clock. But it really is amazing, knowing that all of her nourishment comes directly from me." The baby stopped suckling and looked up at her mother's face. "That's right, Angela. I was talking about you. You are such a pretty baby, yes, you are."

Kristina balanced the now-full basket of baby clothes on her hip, chuckling at her big sister's baby talk. "Your milk must be pure cream. Angela's getting fatter every day. I'm just gonna go put these away next door." Although Angela still slept in the room with Keith and Layla, the guest room would be transformed into a nursery soon. Already, there was a dresser bulging with hand-crocheted blankets and gowns of the softest cotton. Boxes and boxes of tiny diapers to fit a preemie were neatly stacked in the closet.

Layla stopped rocking. "I know you have to go back to school. If Angela was autistic, or is ever diagnosed as being autistic, I would want you for her teacher. I know we'd be keeping you from other children who need you." She pooched out her lower lip. "But we will miss you. Thank you again for giving up your entire Christmas break to spend with us. You've been a phenomenal help."

Deep down, as much as she had enjoyed Kristina and all her help, Layla was also looking forward to things getting back to normal—the *New Normal*. She'd been on bed rest since Thanksgiving, gone into labor prematurely, and had some terrible frights at the hospital before all was well. But now it was time to settle in, just them, Daddy, Mommy, and baby. She smiled as she heard Keith whistling in the kitchen. He'd be going back to his teaching job in a few days too, but he'd been so patient, so understanding through all of this, her main support. Layla glanced up at the calendar. There was a six-week hiatus for what the doctor kept calling "sexual intercourse".

Four more weeks, and she could thank Keith *properly*, she thought with a smile. She was sure Carol and Pops wouldn't mind babysitting.

On the other side of the wall, Kristina put the tiny articles of clothing in the new white dresser. One twin bed had been taken out, replaced with a matching white crib. Perhaps they would leave the other twin bed in case another guest visited, or so that a tired parent could lie down if the baby was sick or fretful. She wouldn't know, never planning to have children herself.

Who would want a perfect, precious, innocent child in my *care, after what they did to me? After they turned me into… this.* Kristina stood and caught a glance of herself in the little lamb-adorned mirror. She knew that Kayla had been shocked; she had seen the expression on her face that first day she arrived. *I don't want them to win. I don't want them to have so much power over me, to change me like this.*

The whole ordeal had been traumatic, from beginning to end. Not that it had ended for her. *Will it ever even, really?* She was torn, wanting to heal, to stand up to them where she was and where she continued to see them, but she also longed for a change, anything to get away from the city where it had happened, put some distance between herself and them.

Being here had been a welcome distraction, but perhaps it was time for a new chapter altogether. Go where no one knew her or might ask questions. She could reinvent herself. She'd miss her students, of course, but they'd be fine. Many of her students had trouble showing their emotions, but they *felt* them. She would explain that a new teacher would be there the next year. New school term, new teacher for them, new students for her.

Kristina shivered a little as she made the decision. As soon as she got home, she'd start applying to another school with a different climate, different everything. And, she decided to look into a counselor. *I've been trying to do it all by myself, and obviously I'm not doing a great job. I can't talk to Kayla—too much to lay on her now.*

A fresh start emotionally, and then a fresh start geographically. *Maybe the mountains. Some rural hammock where nothing bad ever happens.*

It had been a stressful evening. She had come in from the magazine bearing "gifts"—bags of Chinese take-out to remind him of Asahi's cooking—to find Eric completely out of sorts. He blamed it on his arm, but Donna could tell something else was bothering him. Conversation over dinner was tense, with awkward pauses and silences between. After they ate dinner, Donna cleaned up while Eric sat like a lump on the couch, flipping through channels. When Donna insisted they watch a movie on TV, he complied but grumbled, talked over the dialogue, and finally announced that he was going to bed.

After her own ordeal with Lance, Donna had no desire to instigate any romance. *Shouldn't newlyweds have sex every night?* she mused, pouring herself a glass of wine. *Maybe not newlyweds with a broken arm and a recent attack between them.* She'd heard friends talk about the "baggage" someone carried into this relationship or that marriage—now she understood. All of their lifetimes had built up to this very moment, dragging baggage of one kind or another. Some of the baggage was heavier, some lighter, but all of it had an inevitable impact on who they were now. Who they could become together.

She had reckoned on sex being the glue that held them together. They had always gotten along so well, even from the start. They loved one another and wanted to please the other. What could go wrong? She was a journalist as well as a romantic, though, accustomed to looking at the cold, hard facts. She had seen it happen too many times with friends over the years —"perfect" couples who eventually divorced.

In her heart, Donna knew that a strong marriage needed more than sex. More even than what passed for love in most households. She just wasn't sure Eric had "more" to give. She wasn't sure that she did, either—unloading all those memories about her father had, she knew, changed her somehow. She wasn't sure exactly how or why or what it would mean going forward, but she was sure the change for her was positive, cleansing, healing.

Eric's response had not been so positive. Of course, he couldn't read her mind, but after their return, he never brought it up again. He was injured, obviously, but he was also hurting at another level. Or not. *What do I know? We're barely talking.* He seemed content with her taking the lead, dominating, suggesting, instigating. It wasn't that he was wrong, and she was right, but on nights like this one, it felt like she did most of the heavy lifting in the relationship.

Then stop, a voice insisted inside. *Take a step back and see if he steps forward. Give him room.*

Donna put her wine glass in the dishwasher, glancing at the door of the red room as she walked to their bedroom. Since their return from Florida, intimacy had been both less frequent and more "ordinary". Satisfying, though. Lovely. She couldn't complain. There was a valid concern that rough play might delay the healing in his arm, might injure him further. But there definitely seemed to be something else holding Eric back, although she couldn't put her finger on what it was. *Maybe it's just me. Maybe I haven't been sexy enough, or sweet enough, or needy enough.* Stop. *It doesn't have to all be about you.*

In a few minutes, Donna slipped naked and soundlessly between the sheets, snuggling close to Eric's warm back. She put her arm around his waist and listened to his soft breathing as he slept. *Goodnight, wonderful man. I do so love you.*

Suddenly, Eric stirred and picked her arm off his side, pushing it behind him.

"Eric?" she said softly. "Do you need me to get you anything?"

Silence.

For some time, Donna tossed and turned, the first night she could remember when she and Eric had not fallen asleep touching, at least by a hand or a foot. *Was I wrong to tell him about my father? Maybe I shouldn't say anything about Lance, after all. I'll tell Worth, and he'll get fired, and that will be the end of it.*

14

Anti-climactic

Donna was nervous as she stepped into Worth's office. Jessica was already there, too, at her request. They were more than bosses, they were friends. But she was blonde—old stereotypes notwithstanding, she had a well-deserved reputation as being a little flighty. Maybe they wouldn't take her seriously. Perhaps Lance was more of an asset to the magazine than *she* was. Paul said he'd won some awards, anyway. Although Donna had come a long way over the years, dealing with the self-doubts and esteem issues trauma victims face, lately... everything had happened so fast this year. She wasn't sure she had managed to keep pace.

"Come in, come in!" Worth boomed. Handsome in a light gray shirt and signature green tie that matched his eyes, Worth Vincent beckoned for her to sit beside his wife. "How's Eric holding up? Almost out of that cast?" When his mother had purchased the magazine the year before, it had been doing well. Jessica had only been working there a few months. Under Worth's editorial guidance, *Our City* had really flourished. *Jessica's flourished too,* she thought, grateful for her presence.

"Any day now, I think," she told them. There was an

awkward silence, but no one rushed her. Finally, she lifted her head and said, "I don't know where to begin."

Jessica heard the uncharacteristic tremor in her friend's voice and reached out to squeeze Donna's hand. "You can tell us, whatever it is." Her mind was racing. "Eric?"

Donna took a deep breath. "No, no, Eric's fine. It's someone here. The new photographer, Lance Glover. He has been… inappropriate with me several times." Donna's plan was to start at the beginning with a litany of Lance's random comments and innuendos, building up to last night's assault. Although she hadn't been hurt, she had no doubt that without the night watchman's interruption, Lance had intended to molest her, at the very least. At the very worst… the thought made her feel nauseous.

Worth relaxed visibly. He sat back in his chair and shook his head. "Lance Glover no longer works here."

"What?"

"He no longer works here. He sent an email to me last night, quitting. He said that his side gigs are more lucrative than he had anticipated and his job at the magazine is actually holding him back. He even said he would forfeit his next paycheck in lieu of two-weeks' notice." Worth nodded, remembering the initial interview, his work, the email. "Nice fellow, though. Really talented photographer."

When Jessica shot him a look, he cleared his throat. "But obviously, that's no excuse for being inappropriate, talent or no talent. That was always a struggle with Jessica and me, you know. As the boss, I was perhaps more sensitive to what things might sound like or look like than I needed to be, but I'm genuinely sorry Lance said anything out of line." Worth frowned, looking toward a filing cabinet nearby. "As soon as we're through here, I'm going to add a note to his personnel file in case he ever asks for a reference. Any future employer would need to know about this. Thank you for letting me know."

All the wind was out of Donna's sails. She'd pumped herself up for a grand reveal, prepared to drag the guard in to substantiate. There was no need for dramatics. "No, that's okay. I came here instead of HR because you're friends... but if he's gone, he's gone." She managed a smile. "That's a relief, actually." She stood up. "Well, I've got work to do. Sorry to bother you."

After Donna closed the door behind herself, Jessica sat for a moment, silent and frowning.

Worth came around the desk and sat beside her, leaning over to kiss her tenderly. "What is it? You heard her. She's relieved. And Paul can hold down the fort until we find a replacement. Lance finished his last assignment yesterday. The timing works out great for the magazine, in fact."

Jessica shook her head. "It's not that, Worth. I've never seen Donna so... vulnerable, transparent. It's like her wall of giddy perkiness is gone now. She seems different. Not *bad* different, just different. Whatever Lance said or did, obviously has her shaken up." She had a thought. "It might be a good idea if I were to sit in on interviews? Get a female's input? Sometimes our initial impressions are spot on."

Worth chuckled. "I'm glad I passed muster with you. Eventually, anyway! We men can be oafs, that's for sure. With most of us, it's ignorance—we have no idea what we're doing half the time where you ladies are concerned. But there are plenty of others—users. Exploiters. Crude, vulgar. I'm appalled I let one of those guys fly in under the radar." Worth stood and opened the door for his wife. "Keep an eye on her, Jess. We've all been through a lot this year," he said gently. "The Florida job was a lifesaver, but poorly timed. I don't know what I would've done if you'd left right after we got married."

"Or I, you." Jessica came close to him, absentmindedly tickling the top of his shaved head. Every morning now, she made sure there were no errant strands he'd missed. Her hand drifted down to an ear.

He leaned in again. "Whatever are you doing, Mrs. Vincent? We've got work to do, you know." He kissed her, long and hard. Their embrace brought all of their attention and focus onto the moment. "You know, I do have a lock on my door," he said roughly as their hands and lips explored one another.

From around the corner of the wall, they heard a delicate clearing of a throat. They separated. As Jessica smoothed her hair and Worth adjusted his trousers, Skip's head peered inside. "Worth, I just saw the email you copied to me from Lance Glover. Shall I post the job opening online?"

Worth returned to his desk, once again all business. "That'll be fine, Skip—oh, but check with Paul before you do. Maybe he already knows of someone who's looking. I would trust his judgment."

Skip gave him a thumbs-up and grinned at Jessica. The hunger in the room was palpable, and he had stumbled upon many such scenes during the last year. "Sorry to interrupt. Carry on, you little lovebirds!" he said as he stepped out.

Jessica and Worth shared a tender look, but the moment had passed. Jessica had numerous phone calls to make as well as a column to finish. Worth had several other appointments on his schedule before he could even think about taking a break, she knew. She sang out to Skip, "I was just leaving!"

Blowing a kiss at Worth, she walked past Skip and returned to her desk.

Lance Glover had felt it prudent to leave the magazine, but he certainly wasn't ready to leave the city. There were so many photos still to shoot! Some months earlier, he'd stumbled onto a sort of "help wanted" ad in the chat room of one of his favorite porn sites. Not only were photographers needed in his particular area, but the pay mentioned was top notch. There was an element of risk, the kind of photos they wanted required… finesse, patience, sitting in the dark for hours at a time. Once Lance had called the number to discuss it, he was warned that out-and-out stalking might be necessary in order to get the best shots. He had fairly jumped at the opportunity —the job combined his two favorite things: photography and women.

Lance knew there were others out there hoping to cash in on the offer. Soon after he had begun the work, the Peeping Tom reports had started flowing in. No way was he responsible for all the Peeping Tom reports. Perhaps none of them—he was careful. He was professional. He had also gotten distracted from the money somewhere along the line. Looking at things objectively, he realized that he had been too focused on his favorite subject. "Oh, Donnalet. You slipped away too soon," he said out loud as he looked through his photos of her. "All I wanted to do was take your picture in more suitable attire."

He laughed. "Or lack thereof. After I make you a famous model, perhaps you'll *let* me do nice things to you. Donnalet. And if you won't, perhaps I'll do them anyway."

He looked at his watch. Time to grab a bite to eat, then another night of hunting. Now that he wasn't at the magazine office, he'd have to be more strategic where his favorite subject was concerned. He might need help to follow through with Donna Brown. He preferred to work alone, but in this case, he knew a fellow. He called a number on his phone and arranged to meet.

Eric played with the vegetables on his plate. The place wasn't crowded, so he'd taken a booth. He glanced at his left arm, amazed at how free he felt without that damn cast. Fortunately, he'd gotten tan enough before it went on that it hadn't faded *too* badly, he thought. When Donna came home from the club, wouldn't *she* be surprised?

The club. Eric sighed, remembering her wedding night gift that seemed a distant memory. She planned to quit soon, she'd assured him, now that he was back home. But someone had called in sick. Madame X had pleaded for just a little longer? She'd help out this week, anyway. But after... maybe she'd be open to celebrating his newly freed arm in the red room. *Unless the Daddy thing is still an issue.*

He frowned as he cut off a bite of steak and put it in his mouth., barely noticing the taste. Donna was different since Florida. It had taken a lot for her to tell him about her father. And, he had to admit, his response hadn't been overwhelmingly supportive. He'd been appalled that someone would do that to a child, to his own daughter. His thoughts were relentlessly accusing: *You also thought mainly of yourself, how the change of attitude might affect you. Us.* He continued to mentally berate himself until suddenly, his ears pricked up.

Through the slats at the top of the booth behind him, two men were deep in conversation. Eric couldn't hear every word, but what he heard sent a chill down his spine.

"No, I quit," a voice was saying. "No notice, just left. All because of that gorgeous little bitch. I wish I'd pulled every strand of that blonde hair of hers out... or at least..." The voice went too low to understand. "I know she would've complained. Probably did anyway."

A second voice made a comment Eric could not hear.

"...magazine, house, maybe... back now. In no shape... riskier."

More that was inaudible. "The club, yeah."

Eric looked across the diner to the mirror behind the lunch counter. An elderly couple blocked his view of the occupants of the booth, but... *there.* The couple were finished and got up to pay on their way out. Eric could clearly see two men, one in a fishing vest and plaid shirt, the other in camouflage. Perhaps he had been mistaken about them being up to no good. *Those two look like they're about to go camping.*

"She's... tonight. I heard her telling... every night this week. I paid. I'll find some way... until she's outside. Or stop by the house, bare spot in the grass, I've looked in so often." Both men laughed.

Eric watched the mirror out of the corner of his eye in horror as the man in the vest pantomimed a camera. *The Peeping Tom. Maybe both of them are. But what club was a target?* he wondered. His heart began to pound. *Magazine. Club. Blonde.* Surely, they were not discussing Donna? It felt like more than coincidence. He felt nauseous. *What should I do? Should I call 9-1-1? What if I'm wrong?*

Eric left his half-eaten meal and casually walked to the cashier to pay. "Keep the change," he said as he walked out quickly. Inside his car, he waited impatiently with the engine running. He would follow the men just to make sure this had nothing to do with Donna. He had to be mistaken. They were harmless. But if he did happen to see something suspicious, he could call it in then. *Don't get ahead of yourself.*

Ten long minutes later, the two men came out of the diner. Eric's heart sank as one of the men got into a van while the other, into a dark sedan. *Which should I follow?* The decision was made for him when the sedan pulled out into traffic first. Easing in behind it unobstrusively, he followed the car for several blocks before it pulled into a driveway and parked outside an apartment complex. When the man got out, he waved to someone out on a balcony and noisily greeted him. Obviously, *he* was not planning anything furtive any time soon.

The van. Eric put the car into reverse and headed back to the diner. Maybe he hadn't left yet. *Damn.* The van was nowhere in sight. Eric had come there for dinner because it was fairly close by. The apartment was worth a look-see. As he went through the gate of their complex, he slowed down. Eric's eyes darted in every direction, searching for the van. *Nothing.* He circled all of the buildings before he pulled into his parking spot in front of their apartment.

Oh well. Probably nothing. Eric sighed, feeling a bit foolish. On a whim, however, he walked around the end of the building and stopped outside their bedroom window. Hoping that no one had seen him—he might be accused of being the peeper, even outside his own place—Eric pulled out his phone and enabled the flashlight app.

The light revealed nothing near him, but as he moved the phone around, he saw it immediately—a distinct worn area nearer the window. *Donna!*

Eric sped toward the club, hurriedly dialing Donna as he drove. She would have the ringer off, he knew, but prayed she'd feel the vibration and answer. Madame X was strict about certain things, and phones were one of them. It made perfect sense—she didn't want members to come out of a room, see someone with a smartphone, and worry they were being photographed or discussed.

Through the car's Bluetooth, the number rang. And rang. And rang. Eric ended the connection before it went to voice mail. *Damn.* He wasn't even a member at the club. No key. No answer. How would he get inside?

Eric was still blocks away when his phone rang. *Thank God.*

"What's up, babe?" Donna asked. "I had to step outside to use the phone and it's raining. I'm in the car, but I've only got a minute. Why'd you hang up?"

"Don't go back inside, Donna. Stay in the car." Eric sounded out of breath, but his voice was steady.

Donna was alarmed. "What do you mean? What's wrong? Are you okay? I've *got* to go back, babe. I'm the only one here. I'm quitting soon, but it's my jo—"

Eric spoke slowly but firmly as he sat impatient for a red light to flash green. "Have you seen a man there in a fishing vest?"

Despite herself, Donna giggled. The question seemed to come from nowhere. "Noooo. Why? We don't really cater to fi—"

"I think there's a man I saw at the diner on his way. In a fishing vest. I think he may be one of the Peeping Toms." He had a thought as the light changed and he sped off again. "Maybe no vest, but just a plaid shirt." *What if he changes first?* He suddenly felt ridiculous. A damn good stonemason, yes, but what gave him the idea he was fucking Sherlock Holmes?

Donna twisted around in her seat just as she saw the front door closing. "Oh, damn. I've got to go, babe. A member just went inside, and I need to check them in. Bye! Be home in a few hours."

Holding her purse over her head to shield her from the rain, Donna let herself back inside. *Hmm. No one waiting after all.* Only she and Madame X had a master key... and then she remembered the trouble about her key that second night. She had looked high and low, distraught that she had lost it, only to find it on her desk the next morning at work. She assumed it had fallen from her purse and been covered up with papers. *Had someone taken it, made a copy, then returned the original? Who would* do *that?*

Donna rounded the corner of the hallway just as an arm could be seen pulling shut a door. In the dim lighting, she could still see enough to incriminate. *Plaid. Oh man. What should I do?*

Madame X was with a client and therefore unavailable. Interrupting her at work could have disastrous consequences. But rule or no rule, she needed to let Eric know. "Eric," she hissed into the phone when she returned to the lobby, "I think he's here. The man in the plaid shirt."

"Open the front door for me," Eric replied. "I just got here."

"Now what?" she whispered. They stood in the semi-darkness, unsure of the best way to handle the situation, if there even was a situation. "He might have someone in there, Eric, someone we'd embarrass to no end. He *might* be someone completely innocent of anything but wearing a plaid shirt to an S & M club. We can't just burst in on him!"

"No, but we could wait for him to come out and then follow him, I guess. Discreetly. Maybe this is a stop on his way to… peeping. Or he's escalated. Tired of just watching through windows and ready to take it to another level. Maybe he's brought a victim here."

Donna snorted quietly. "You've been watching too much TV," she grumbled. Pause. "But that *would* be horrible."

They were still discussing their options when the silent club phone glowed red, signifying a call from someone on the premises. "Lemme grab this," Donna said quietly. She cleared her throat softly and assumed her friendly phone voice. "May I help you?"

It was a man. "I'm having a little difficulty with some of the equipment. I-I'm new at this, and there's some gizmo here that seems to be stuck. I was trying to fix it and the lights went off. Could someone take a look?" There was a low laugh. "I'm still decent."

Donna rolled her eyes and mouthed the word "repair" for

Eric's benefit. "Of course. I'll be right there—what room are you in?"

Eric couldn't hear the voice at the other end, but even in the relative darkness, he recognized Donna's reaction for what it was—fear. She softly placed the receiver back in its cradle. "That was him. Plaid Man. What should I do? What do I say to him?"

Eric straightened his back. The man he had overheard in the diner was here. From what little he could make out, the man knew Donna. There had definitely been someone looking in their window from outside. He had mimed cameras. The man just feet away from him, he believed, intended to do her harm. But what proof was there? They could call the police, but what exactly could they tell the dispatcher? Could he risk ruining Madame X's club because of a feeling, a guess, a hunch?

"Give me the key," he whispered. "I'll go."

Breathing hard, Eric turned the key in the door; it opened into darkness. The door slammed shut and he heard the lock reengage.

The light went on again as a voice said, "Thank you for —*oof!*"

Eric's fist made contact with the man's jaw, pushing him hard into the door. He was indeed wearing a plaid shirt. It was indeed the man from the diner. "You're not exactly what I had in mind," he said calmly, rubbing his jaw. "But I don't mind getting rough if you don't."

Standing in the hallway, Donna could only guess what was taking place. The walls were soundproof. Her imagination was running wild. *What is taking so long?* After an agonizing amount of time, the door finally opened. Eric, bruised and bloody but smiling grimly, nodded for her to come inside. "Do you know this guy?"

Lance Glover, bound by both ankles and wrists, hung on a

St. Andrew's cross. His nose appeared to have been broken; his shirt was torn. "Donnalet!" he cried out. "I think there's been a misunderstanding. This *prick* thinks I've come here to hurt you. Nothing could be further from the truth. Nothing! I want to make you famous."

"This is the guy from work!" Donna exclaimed. "The jerk! The photographer!" She stepped closer to him. "He grabbed me the other night when I worked late, and Lord only knows what he would've done if the guard hadn't come in—"

Eric embraced her. "He grabbed you? Why didn't you tell me? Never mind; we can deal with that later. So what do we do with him now?"

Donna crossed her arms. "I know what I'd *like* to do." She walked over to a little table and picked up a whip. "Were you planning to use this on me tonight, Lance?"

Lance shook his head as vehemently as the choke collar would permit. "I've done nothing wrong. I was *going* to do nothing wrong. I just wanted to take some photos. You weren't cooperative. There was an order for photos of a woman with curly blonde hair; that's all. Someone out there likes your 'type'. Of course, I agree with him. You could have—"

Eric's blow to Lance's stomach shut him up, but to his credit, the man recovered quickly. "That's it. I'm pressing charges. I'll have the club closed down and see you both in jail. I'm a *member* here. I have a *right* to be here. I *paid* to be here."

Just then, Donna noticed Lance's padded backpack in a corner. As she walked in its direction, she cooed, "So, there's nothing naughty on your camera?"

For the first time, the man on the cross looked frightened. His face drained of color, contorted in horror. "You can't do that; you can't see. That's my personal property. Stop! No!"

He continued to plead with her as she slowly, even coyly, removed the camera from the bag. "Ooh, look," she murmured. "A camera. Lance has a big, big camera. Now let me see. How does it turn on? Oh, there it is. Well, what do you know? Pictures of women taken through their windows! Hmm. I think the police will be quite happy to look at all your wor—" Donna froze as she scrolled through more images.

There were dozens of photographs of her. There she was at work, in the parking garage, bending over to pick something up, on the phone, laughing at lunch. She gasped. *What the fuck?* At the apartment, too. Naked, getting dressed, talking on the phone in her FaceTime costumes. He had obviously been stalking her for months. Without a word, never taking her eyes off the man on the cross, she handed the camera to Eric.

The camera had re-set to the beginning. He scowled as he thought of all of those women around the city, blithely going on about their business without a clue that they were being watched. Photographed. Their privacy invaded, their images virtually raped by this man. When he came to the first photo of Donna, he looked no further. With an anguished cry, he held the camera high over his head, as if to throw it against the wall.

Both Lance and Donna screamed in unison, "Don't!"

"My work!" Lance pleaded. "My camera! That's worth a lot of money. You have no right."

"The cops!" Donna cried. "It's proof." She walked to Eric and laid a hand on his arm to calm him. She had never seen him so angry. She wasn't sure he could even hear her, so intent was he on destroying the camera with its vile contents.

Slowly, he lowered the camera and pulled out his phone. "Yes, I'd like to report a Peeping Tom," he said quietly, giving the club address. "What? No. Trust me, he's not going anywhere."

15

All is Well

The hearing for Lance Glover was well-attended. When word got out at the magazine that one of their own, or who had *been* one of their own, would stand before a judge, Worth announced that anyone wanting to be there could have the day off. Although he had done nothing wrong in the hiring process, he still felt responsible at some level. The least he could do was appear in court, answer any questions the judge might have, and restrain Eric if it came to that. Donna had described the events leading to Lance's arrest, and Worth secretly wished that Eric had taken more liberties with the troll.

Newspaper headlines simply read *Peeper in Custody*. Every scared woman and indignant husband came out of the woodwork for the spectacle. Just as the community had breathed a corporate sigh of relief when Jessica had identified the arsonist last year, it now breathed another for a little while, at least for now. Rumor had it that Lance Glover could identify other Peeping Toms in the city and was anxious to cooperate with the authorities. A plea bargain was on the table, but all that would be decided later.

Today, Judge William Tate eyed the full house in his courtroom, wishing he'd gotten the haircut his wife had been
nagging him about for weeks. The Peeping Tom case would be
in the news and *stay* in the news, possibly for a very long time.
The judge smiled. It was an election year.

His wife had issued clear orders at breakfast: no way should
that horrible man be free on bail. The judged squirmed in his
seat. Although there were multiple infractions, Lance Glover
had no prior arrests. Under the law, there wasn't much wiggle
room. But there was some.

Donna happened to be looking at Judge Tate when the
bailiff handed him a folded note. The judge opened it, his
mouth moving a little as he read. Grimly, he nodded and said
something to the bailiff, who headed off in a hurry, his purpose
unrevealed to the courtroom.

When the time came, Judge Tate addressed the accused,
"Lance Glover, you have been charged with voyeurism, inva-
sion of privacy, petit theft, assault, and the sale or distribution
of pornography. How do you plead?"

Lance Glover displayed none of the bravado he'd shown at
the magazine—a few nights in county lock-up can be educa-
tional—but he spoke loudly and clearly, "Not guilty, your
honor." The spectators responded with various catcalls and
boos, necessitating the judge's use of his gavel.

When the room was quiet again, the Assistant District
Attorney asked the judge to consider Glover a flight risk. He
had no family in the area and had recently quit his job, he said,
waving vaguely in Worth's direction. The judge took it all in.
The magazine. Maybe they would like to do a feature on him?
Good publicity…

The public defender was about to put in her own two cents
when one of her assistants handed her another folded note.

She conferred with Glover and then addressed the judge. "There are protesters outside the courtroom, Your Honor. Mr. Glover is happy to stay in protective custody. Request for bail is withdrawn."

After sitting in jail for several weeks, despite the numerous allegations, Lance Glover never stood trial. As expected, he pled out, alerting the police to several other enterprising photographers in the city he knew to be operating currently for the benefit of a particular online pornographer—some professional, like him, others, amateurs. In exchange for his testimony, he was granted five years' probation—in another city. A group of women also filed a class action civil suit, winning a nice settlement.

Madame X's club did not suffer at all from the eventful night with Eric and Lance. There was an upgrade to the security system—keypads rather than keys—and Madame X hired full-time staff to maintain safety and privacy for her clients. It was rumored that Lance had installed tiny hidden cameras, which Madame X never confirmed or denied. She did, however, assure her clients that after a brief closure, the club had passed a thorough inspection and was open for business. There was, if anything, an uptick in membership.

It was a beautiful spring day in the city, sunny with a cool breeze announcing that they might have a few more days of sweater weather before things heated up. Eric met Donna downtown for lunch—he was building ornate stone columns outside an office park nearby. They sat and enjoyed hot dogs by the fountain as they had done the first day they met.

Today, Jessica and Worth joined them. The four often spent time together these days, and Jessica was impressed by how much more outgoing her ex-boyfriend was. Whatever influence Donna had had, the results were positive. Donna still seemed to be more fragile, but every day saw improvement. And maybe fragile was the wrong word, Jessica decided. There was something she needed, though. She hoped her friend would get it.

While Eric conversed with Worth on any number of topics, Jessica and Donna compared baby photos on their phone. Between Angela's family and the adopted extras, the baby lacked for nothing. Layla and Keith were completely comfortable spending a date night out while Jessica and Worth, Chet and Carol, Kari and Jon, or Donna and Eric babysat. They rotated Friday evenings, besides family gatherings and impromptu visits. Angela thrived with all the attention.

"I swear, she's the cutest baby ever," Donna gushed. "I told Layla she should take her to a photographer, sign her up for modeling. Those baby ads in the magazine have got nothing on her."

Jessica agreed. "Paul's going over this week, in fact. He has friends in the 'biz' as he put it. Who knows where it will lead? She could be the new face of baby food, diapers, or Baby Gap." She grinned mischievously over her hot dog. "I mean, *you* were going to be a model, so…"

Donna laughed and threw a French fry at her friend before her smile turned into a frown. "You have no idea how horrifying that was, to see myself on that perv's camera. I just hope all the video from the club was destroyed along with the files. We found a camera in every room. Every. Room."

Jessica raised her eyebrows. "So you and Eric may have starred in some smash hits without knowing it?" She knew by now that Donna's interest in the club pre-dated her job there.

Donna made a face. "There was that one night. But let's

just say we may have and leave it at that. Anyway, we're not members there. Our room at home will suffice. The club brings back bad memories."

"Ah yes, the infamous red room!" The first time Jessica and Worth had eaten dinner at Donna and Eric's apartment, she'd opened the red room door by accident, thinking it was the bathroom. Of course, they had to get the whole story—the bullet version, anyway.

On the way home, Jessica had brought it up again to Worth. Was that something he thought he would enjoy? A red room? The outfits? The toys?

Worth had shaken his head. "Different strokes for different folks, love. And you already 'stroke' me just fine." To encourage her, he grabbed her hand and placed it in his lap as he drove.

"You don't fantasize about other things? I mean, I'm willing to do *just* about anything you want," Jessica had offered, her hand exploring. "Within reason."

Worth chuckled. "Don't you know me better than that? I know we haven't been married all that long, but seriously? Let's see, I'm going to quiz you. What size shoes do I wear?"

"Twelve narrow."

"Okay. That was an easy one. What's my favorite color?"

"Green. Like your eyes."

"Correct again. And what, pray tell, is my favorite ice cream flavor?"

"Vanilla." The look on his face when she said the word was priceless. "You mean…"

Worth had pulled into the condo garage, shut the car off, and taken Jessica's face in his hands. "I mean that I could not care less if anyone thinks we are 'vanilla', or even if we are. If handcuffs and whips bring pleasure to other folks, great. There is no need to compare ourselves to anyone else. I love you; you love me. And when you get right down to it, what goes on behind closed doors is no one's business."

Jessica's hand had drifted further down as they embraced in the front seat. "Well, hello big guy," she said with an appreciative murmur. "I think those closed doors are about to see some action."

Worth had twisted his head this way and that. The parking garage was, for the moment, empty except for them and empty, parked cars. It was late and therefore unlikely anyone would be leaving the complex. "Do you remember what you told me about wanting it all," he'd murmured as he played with her hair. "Way back when we were prim and proper and only talked each night on the phone?"

Jessica had laughed softly. "That roller coaster ride! Of course, I remember. You commented that I wanted to make sweet, sweet, soulmate love on Sunday afternoons after church—"

Worth had put a finger on her lips to interrupt. "And you said you *also* wanted to make mad monkey love in the back seat of the car in an airport parking garage." He looked around and then looked at her with a leer. "This isn't the airport, but—"

In response, Jessica had scrambled over the seat without hesitation.

———

Eric finished washing up after dinner while Donna sat at her laptop, scrolling through real estate. Eric's stone work had paid so well since Christmas that they could actively search for a house. Large enough for a family one day and a better-equipped red room now. They still divided their lovemaking between the bedroom and playroom, but thankfully, Lance Glover had not made a huge difference in their relationship.

Eric's response had impressed Donna—his concern, protectiveness, strength, even his anger. He had been forceful that night. She had wanted to tell him in a way that he could understand, but finally, the night before, she had poured her heart out.

"I never had that kind of concern and protection from my father," she had told him through her tears. "I didn't know how badly I needed it until that night, when you took charge like that. It was like everything from before, my anger, my hunger to be cared for, it all just melted away. All I could see was *you*. Until that night, I'd never realized how deeply I needed to feel that way. You really came through for me."

Eric had hugged her tightly, wiping her face gently. She had drifted off to sleep entwined in the security of their love for one another, the assurance that can be both aphrodisiac and sedative. But long after Donna had gone to sleep, Eric lay awake thinking. Planning. Tonight, he was ready.

"Well, that's it for the kitchen, babe," he said lightly, wiping his hands on a towel. "I'm fixing myself a drink; would you care for one?"

"None for me, thanks," Donna said absently. Intent on square footage and backyards, she didn't notice Eric step into the red room and close the door behind himself.

Several minutes later, he cracked open the door and called to her. "Could you come here a minute, babe?"

Donna waved at the door, annoyed. "Not now, there's a new development near the river I want to check ou—"

"I said to *come here*!" Eric's voice was surprisingly firm. He stood in the doorway, fully clothed, as he pulled his longish hair back into a ponytail. Then he waited, hands on his hips. Just standing there.

Donna closed the laptop meekly. "Do you want me to change into my boots or anything?"

"I said to *come here*."

When she obeyed, Eric closed the door. Candles were already lit around the room, making their shadows dance on the walls and ceiling. Restraints were attached to the bed in a variety of configurations. Music played in the background, softly enough that it wasn't a distraction, but loudly enough to evoke mood. *That's new*, Donna thought. The symphonic arrangement had an air of mystery, even danger.

"Undress."

Without a word, Donna took her clothes off, amazed at how shy she suddenly felt. This was her *husband*. This was her *sub*, for crying out loud! Tonight, though, he was someone else. *He* was the Dom, and it was quite apparent that he no longer needed to be "talked through" the process.

Eric said nothing as Donna eased her t-shirt over her head and slipped out of her shorts. She stood there in her lace bra and panties, still wondering at some level if he was going to ask her to take over from there. He held up an accusing finger and made a little noise deep in his throat, warning her. "Keep going."

Slowly, Donna reached behind her back to unhook her bra, letting it fall to the carpet. She reached down and wiggled out of her panties. Standing in front of the still-clothed Eric, she felt unusually small and vulnerable. The music, however, was suddenly bigger. It seemed to be getting louder, more intense. Donna's heart beat faster. Her excitement was building, that kind of leaning forward down there. A little drip of moisture ran unchecked down one thigh. *And we haven't even started.*

Eric sat on the bed and pulled her across his lap. "I can hold you as strongly as restraints," he said, pinning her naked legs with one of his, a vise grip on both her hands above her head with his left hand. "You have been bad, Donna." *Whack.* "You wanted more, but you didn't tell me." *Whack.* "You *needed* more, but you didn't speak up." *Whack.*

On and on, the spanking continued, each blow landing a little harder than the one previous as the music swelled. Just when she wondered if this was *all* that was going to happen here—this punishment—he stopped. Pulling her to her feet, Eric backed her against the closed door.

"I know what you want. I know what you've wanted from our first night in here. You told me, but I wasn't listening." Eric pinned her shoulder to the door with one hand, as he unzipped his pants with the other. When he took his hand away from her shoulder, his weight against her body still trapped her. He fumbled below his waist, releasing his erection to press against her. A wave of desire shivered through her as his heat almost burned her skin.

"Are you ready for me?" he murmured.

Donna's affirmative came out part-moan, part-squeak. The music was building and building, mirrored by their increasingly heavy breaths. Eric threw her to the bed, face down, her legs dangling over the side. Entering her as he pulled her torso off the bed, he thrust slowly and deeply. She felt like a doll in his hands, powerless to move, helpless to change position so that she might benefit from his movements. His thrusts became faster, deeper. *He'll climax, and then it will be over,* she thought, her heart sinking. *I can't... not like this.* For reasons she could not explain, she felt as lonely as she had ever felt. And there was nothing she could do to help herself.

Suddenly, Eric moved out of her and in one swift move, turned her over and off the bed and reached behind Donna's back, grabbing her buttocks. He rested her back again on the door, groaning as he entered her again. Donna wrapped her legs around him; he allowed her the space to move and they began to rock against the hard surface. The feel of her skin against his shirt, her hands on his bare buttocks in contrast, almost sent her to the edge.

Faster, faster, deeper as the music swelled to its crescendo... "*Aaiihh,*" Donna screamed as she reached her climax with Eric. When he started to disengage, she screamed again, "No! Please, no! Don't stop!"

Eric pressed her harder against the door. With another groan of ecstasy, she bucked against him, her legs flying up. For the first time in her life, her orgasm brought on a great sob from deep inside of her.

As her climax slowly melted into bliss, Eric laid her down gently. Supporting himself on one elbow, he used his free arm to cuddle her bent legs into his lap before softly wiping her tears away. "Shh, sweet Donna. Don't cry. Don't cry." Had he misunderstood? Had she not wanted this? Old insecurities threatened.

Donna's sniffling eased. The music also slowed, got quieter. *Why have we never had music before? I really like that.*

Eric lay back on the bed beside her as the next movement of a symphony sounded its opening notes, a more soothing melody. "Donna?" he whispered.

"Yes," she said.

He sat up again so that he could kiss her. "Just tell me. I've been selfish, thinking only of pleasing myself. Tonight, was it—"

"A gift to me," she whispered. "Let's spend the rest of our lives giving each other gifts like this, never holding back, never assuming. Telling each other exactly what we need and want—"

"And meeting that need or want completely. Any time—" he continued.

"Any place," Donna whispered.

"Any way."

They said the last line in unison, "Only you."

Halloween News

Autumn may have painted the leaves outside a thousand shades of red, orange, brown and gold, but inside Worth and Jessica's house on a hill overlooking both city and river, the fireplace roared, banishing any chill in the air that had managed to enter whenever a new guest arrived. Eric's handiwork had been one of his favorite jobs. He and Donna had spent many a happy Saturday with the Vincents, talking and laughing as they worked. Donna had become a helpful assistant, making his weekend jobs fly by.

The house was built to the Vincents' specs. First-time guests oohed and ahhed over the fireplace as they sampled appetizers and drank wine. Jessica had decorated subtly for the party, but the food was appropriately Halloween-themed, much to the delight of the children present. Paul and Skip had adopted a little boy from China. A few of the magazine staff had brought their kids. Angela Henderson toddled around in a mermaid outfit whenever she wasn't on Grandma Carol or Poppa Chet's lap.

Three years earlier, Carol had managed to change her daughter's mind about choosing a wedding date that commemorated her first encounter with Worth at a Halloween party, wisely pointing out that they would soon tire of spending every anniversary handing out candy to neighborhood children. They had been married on November first, instead. Tonight's party celebrated both All Hallowed Eve and their third anniversary.

Jessica wore the same costume each year—the same style, anyway. Wonder Woman had given birth to precious Lily eighteen months ago—now playing blocks happily in one corner with her Chinese buddy as his proud daddies supervised. She was pregnant again with what the doctor advised would be a son. She had given up finding a ready-made costume that would fit and sewed one herself. "At least my old boots fit," she laughed as she waddled happily around the room.

"Hey, Kristina called to tell me that she and hubby may make it for Christmas," Layla said as she adjusted little Angela's "tail". "She said the mountains are beautiful in the winter. Maybe we'll go there instead."

"How is she doing, really?" Kayla had raved about the transformation she saw in her little sister. Everyone had been concerned about the shy young woman when she came to help with the baby, but since then, her life, her job, her attitude, even her appearance, had completely changed. Visits since then had been filled with exuberance, with joy. And why not? After some trials and tribulations, she'd married the man of her dreams, just as Jessica had.

Jessica waved across the room to Darth Vader, also known as her husband. He liked to pop his helmet on as he dispensed candy at the door, but otherwise left it on the foyer table. After motioning for sister-in-law Kari to take over candy duties, he threw his arms around Jessica for a quick kiss. Rubbing her prominent belly, he smiled. "My arms won't be able to reach around you for much longer. You really are a wonder, Wonder Woman."

Jessica patted her stomach. "We have living proof that the force is with *you*." She giggled.

Overhearing the exchange, Donna, newly arrived with Eric, groaned loudly. "*So* corny!" she exclaimed. Dressed as a dominatrix, she confided to Jessica that she hadn't had time to look for an actual costume. "But looky here—I want to give you something. It's an anniversary present."

Jessica hugged her friend as she took the oblong box, festive in Halloween colors. The Browns had moved into the development first, a few blocks over, about the time Lily was born. Last summer, they'd moved into their own home. She loved being so close, able to share meals, watch movies together occasionally. "Shall I unwrap it now?"

"Not yet. In here." Donna led her into the kitchen area, where they would have more privacy. "The traditional gift for third anniversaries *is* leather, so I am dressed appropriately for the occasion."

Jessica squealed with laughter as she pulled out a leather riding crop. "I may have to hide this for a few months," she said, "or little Greg in here might wonder what in the world is going on!"

The women hugged again before Jessica retrieved a fresh bottle of Chardonnay from the refrigerator. She was having juice, of course, doctor's orders, but their other guests could partake. Holding it up, she asked, "Is Chardonnay okay with you? There's Merlot in the living room, if you'd prefer."

Donna blushed. "Just juice for me, thank you," she said quietly.

The unspoken meaning of her answer hung in the air as Donna beamed. Jessica's eyes grew wide. "What the what? Are you and Eric—"

"As a matter of fact, I'm due about three months after you," Donna exclaimed as Jessica led the way back to the party.

"I'm counting on lots of hand-me-downs." She laughed. "You've got me covered, since you've got one of each."

Donna held back, enjoying the festive scene. Bits of mica in the river rock fireplace she had helped Eric build glittered in the firelight. She nodded across the room at Carol and Chet, like parents to her now, understanding, always lending an ear when needed. They had entered a second chapter of life together after losing their spouses to accident and disease. She hoped it would be a long, happy chapter ahead.

Layla and Keith, Kari and Jon, Jessica and Worth, even Kristina and her mountain man. Each couple had a story to tell, but she hoped for the same conclusion: Love finds a way. Love lasts.

The smile on her face caught Eric's eye as he closed the front door after passing out treats. Zigzagging through chattering guests, he took her in his arms. Beneath her leathers and boots, she'd worn a t-shirt and leggings, so she didn't reveal *too* much to the crowd; he was dressed as a lumberjack. His hair and beard were long over the buffalo plaid flannel shirt, jeans inside knee-high boots, and the fake ax that hung from his belt.

"You're looking especially sexy this evening," he murmured in her ear. "Pregnancy suits you."

"Tell me again when I start showing. A big belly may interfere with… some activities."

Eric chuckled. "Well then. Whaddaya say we enjoy a great deal of shenanigans before that happens. Starting tonight."

Donna reached up to kiss him. "Keep the clothes on," she whispered, "but lose the ax."

THE END

Emily Sharpe

Emily Sharpe is the pen name for a writer, editor and illustrator in south Florida. A former newspaper columnist, she loves to travel and perform in community theater. Mother of four and grandmother of five, Emily substitute teaches, sings, volunteers in the community and attends a raucous group of writers once a month called "Use Your Words." She heartily believes in love and finding one's joy – and she hopes you enjoy this story of romance. Readers may contact her by e-mail: emilysharpebooks@gmail.com.

Don't miss these exciting titles by Emily Sharpe and Blushing Books!

Dear Editor
The Stonemason and the Lady

Blushing Books

Blushing Books is one of the oldest eBook publishers on the web. We've been running websites that publish spanking and BDSM related romance and erotica since 1999, and we have been selling eBooks since 2003. We hope you'll check out our hundreds of offerings at http://www.blushingbooks.com.

Blushing Books Newsletter

Please join the Blushing Books newsletter
to receive updates & special promotional offers.
You can also join by using your mobile phone:
Just text BLUSHING to 22828.